ABDUCTION COLD CASE

CONNIE QUEEN

LOVE INSPIRED SUSPENSE

INSPIRATIONAL ROMANCE

LOVE INSPIRED® SUSPENSE
INSPIRATIONAL ROMANCE

Recycling programs
for this product may
not exist in your area.

ISBN-13: 978-1-335-58809-8

Abduction Cold Case

Love Inspired
22 Adelaide St. West, 41st Floor
Toronto, Ontario M5H 4E3, Canada
www.LoveInspired.com

Printed in U.S.A.

Who would care if a kidnapping cold case were being investigated?

The kidnapper would. But how would someone know she was meeting Mrs. Barclay?

Silas and Kennedy made their way through the woods to the north, to where the trees thinned. Somewhere to the left, headlights shone through the trees. The gunman was still coming their way.

Headlights bore down on them, and the truck's engine roared. The driver was going to ram them.

"Go. Go."

A concrete pole stood in the middle of the road, supposedly to create a barrier for people not to enter, but Silas swung the ATV around the barricade and onto the rickety bridge.

The farther they went, the more the rotted boards sagged and bowed. She turned to see if the gunman had followed, but he'd stopped at the entrance.

Silas slowed the ATV.

"What's wrong?" She leaned over to look around him. At least three boards were missing.

A shot blasted through the air, and something whizzed past her ear.

"Keep your head down and hang on tight." Silas backed up a few feet and then floored it...

Connie Queen has spent her life in Texas, where she met and married her high school sweetheart. Together they've raised eight children and are enjoying their grandchildren. Today, as an empty nester, Connie lives with her husband and her Great Dane, Nash, and is working on her next suspense novel.

Books by Connie Queen

Love Inspired Suspense

Justice Undercover
Texas Christmas Revenge
Canyon Survival
Abduction Cold Case

Visit the Author Profile page at LoveInspired.com.

I am crucified with Christ: nevertheless I live;
yet not I, but Christ liveth in me: and the life which I
now live in the flesh I live by the faith of the Son of God,
who loved me, and gave himself for me.
—*Galatians* 2:20

This book is dedicated with lots of love
to my oldest daughter, Andi, who is always willing to
read my stories and tell me what she really thinks.
Not only are you a hard worker, but a great mom to your
five kids and wife to Clint. So glad you could move closer
to "home." Keep encouraging those kiddos. Love you.

ONE

Kennedy Wells slammed on the brakes of her Mini Cooper as she looked out the driver's-side window and squinted toward the dense woods.

Was that yellow she saw among the foliage? Yeah, there was a house back there. Finally! She put her car into Reverse and backed up until she was even with the overgrown drive.

She was thirty miles from the closest town of Liberty on a gravel road—if she could even call it a road—that ran along the Texas side of the Red River. She had driven by the entrance three times before noticing the tiny speck of color. The house sat a hundred yards from the entrance, hidden among giant oaks, pecans and cedars. Even though the leaves had fallen, the cedars huddled together, towering among the others, making the home virtually undetectable from the road. Now she was twenty minutes late for her appointment.

Hopefully, this meeting wouldn't take long

because she hated driving at night in areas she wasn't familiar with.

The case had been a strange one ever since Kennedy received the mysterious file two days ago. An envelope addressed to her at Bring the Children Home Project, where Kennedy volunteered as a psychologist, was on her desk when she came in that morning. The small volunteer organization helped families locate their missing child or find the faith to cope with losing one. Since her normal job at Stone River Counseling was closed for renovations until next week, she'd decided to spend more time on the cases at Bring the Children Home. Sometimes the organization took on cold cases if requested by a family member or a law enforcement agency, depending on the current caseload.

But this file just showed up on her desk with no return address or name of sender. Strange.

The Manila folder contained old newspaper clippings and copies of legal documents about the kidnapping of a three-year-old girl, Harper Barclay, from a local park.

After looking over the twenty-six-year-old local cold case and discussing it with her supervisor, her boss decided to have Kennedy interview the mom of the child to see if there were any updates. When she called Elizabeth Barclay, the victim's mother, she eagerly agreed to an appointment.

Kennedy wondered if the mom had been the one to send the file. And if so, why address it to her when she was relatively new to the organization?

As she pulled in, her gaze landed on the rusty tricycle peeking out from the thick stand of milkweeds next to a fallen cedar tree. Dread seeped through Kennedy's soul, and her chest squeezed. She eased off the accelerator, and the Mini Cooper rolled to a stop.

The winter sun set low above the horizon, shadows falling fast, but the riding toy looked the same as the one in the photo that was included in the file.

Had the mother let the plaything sit for all these years?

Maybe Harper had left it sitting in that exact spot. But for twenty-six years? Surely not. Kennedy tried to imagine what it must be like for a mother to have her daughter abducted—kidnapped at the park while she took her younger child to the restroom. How many times had the mother awoken only to replay the scene in her head, wishing—pleading—for a do-over?

Kennedy's gaze swept across the rest of the property, trying to get a good feel for the place before darkness overtook her. The clothesline sagged under the weight of a faded quilt, shouting welcome better than any sign. Orange and yellow mums overflowed the window boxes, and a pair of wooden rocking chairs facing the west on the wraparound porch completed the serene scene. Even the leaning swing set in the side yard evoked the image of *home*. All it was lacking was Christmas lights and decorations.

The dark silhouettes of horses and Texas longhorns grazed in a nearby pasture.

The country setting looked like the perfect place to raise a child, which made Kennedy's visit even more painful.

What atrocities plagued the little girl after her abduction? Was she even still alive? The thought tied her stomach into knots.

A strange feeling Kennedy couldn't pinpoint gripped her—like she'd been here before. Probably the feeling was brought on because she'd studied the pictures numerous times over the last forty-eight hours. The tricycle once again tugged at her attention. She reached into her satchel and pulled out the photograph of three-year-old Harper Barclay sitting on the toy—a gleeful grin firmly in place, brown hair blowing across her face. The cedar tree in the photo was just a stump now. Even though the picture was a tad blurry, the girl's happiness was obvious.

The time on the car's dashboard read three minutes past eight. She finished pulling forward and stopped behind an older-model sedan. Kennedy grabbed her small backpack containing her notes from the passenger seat, a notepad and her cell phone so she could record the conversation.

She inhaled the smell of damp earth and cedar—a scent that produced a calming effect on her. As she approached the front door, she noted it stood ajar a couple of inches. Mrs. Barclay was expecting her. She'd probably left it cracked so she could hear Kennedy approach. There was no doorbell, thus she rapped on the side of the house.

A dog barked somewhere in the home. After a few seconds, she knocked again. When no one answered, Kennedy took a step inside of the entryway and half closed the door so the warm air wouldn't escape. Her eyes were slow to adjust to the darkness. "Mrs. Barclay. I'm here."

Again, ferocious barking came from a back room. Besides the animal, there was no other sound in the house.

Where was Mrs. Barclay? Hopefully she hadn't forgotten their appointment. Maybe she should've called to let her know she was running late.

"Mrs. Barclay. It's Kennedy Wells from Bring the Children Home Project. I'm here to talk about Harper's cold case." She moved farther inside and into the kitchen when her gaze went to papers strewn on the counter. A cookie jar lay shattered in pieces on the tile floor.

Something was wrong.

A heavy pounding accompanied the agitated barking, like the dog was jumping against the door.

Muffled noises sounded from her left—the opposite direction from the dog. Kennedy stood frozen in place, her gaze trying to make out the black shadows. Being a psychologist, she didn't normally attend the recovery of children, but instead visited with the family in a safe environment. She grabbed her cell phone from her pocket, but her hands shook so badly she dropped the phone. It hit the kitchen mat before disappearing under the stove. In a panic, she reached into her backpack and her fingers touched hard plastic. Her lipstick-sized Mace. She silently removed the agent. Temptation to turn on a light was strong, but she didn't want to make her location known.

A crash sounded in another room, followed by a groan.

Kennedy jumped. *Get out of the house and go for help.* As she took a step back toward the entryway, a shadow moved into the room.

She swallowed down the urge to scream and

edged closer to the wall, hopefully melting into the shadows. Heavy footsteps crossed the living room and moved toward the kitchen. She crouched down.

The incessant barking made her nerves crawl. *Please, God, don't let the man see me.*

"Shut up, stupid dog, before I come back there," a masculine voice yelled. Something whizzed across the room and hit a metal display rack in the entryway. The shelf toppled to the floor, blocking the front door.

He was moving her way. With her heart pounding in her ears, she stayed low and crept along the cabinets as quietly as possible. She didn't breathe. Her shoe slipped on a cookie and caused her knee to bump into the cabinet.

A second later, a masked man holding a tire iron stepped around the kitchen corner. Their eyes locked. Despite the shadows, she could make out his black eyes.

As she stood and started to run, she pointed the Mace and screamed, "Help! Help!"

Before she could push the button, he grabbed her arm as she went to go around the counter, his fingers biting into her flesh. His position put him between her and the front door.

"Ow." Retaining her grip on the spray, she jerked out of his grasp and dashed through the living room, toward the bedrooms and the dog.

Just as she twisted the doorknob, metal smashed into the doorframe. Wooden splinters flew into the air, a few stabbing her. She threw the door open and then spun, spraying the Mace.

"Agh." The man's hands flew to his face. "I'm gonna…kill you for that."

Before she could respond, a blur of brown whizzed past her and leaped into the man. Fueled by adrenaline, she lost her balance and fell against the door, barely keeping her footing. The Mace tumbled to the floor.

The biggest dog Kennedy had ever seen latched onto the man's arm and shook ferociously.

"Get down," the man screamed. "Stop."

The house was dark, but Kennedy took off, making out the path leading through the living room. She bolted to the opposite end of the home and ran into a room and closed the door. She didn't know the layout of the residence, but the moonlight cast enough light to see a bed. Noises from within the house continued as the man wrestled with the dog. Glancing around, she tried to find a weapon. She felt along the wall when suddenly her foot bumped into something soft. Before her eyes focused, she knew what she would see.

A body lay on the floor. A woman.

Kennedy knelt beside the female and leaned over. She recognized Mrs. Barclay from an interview the woman had conducted with a local television station on the twenty-year anniversary of Harper's abduction. A faint breath brushed Kennedy's cheek.

"Mrs. Barclay?" she whispered.

The woman didn't move. A dark line stretched across her forehead. Kennedy got up and flipped the light switch up, but everything remained dark. She returned to Mrs. Barclay's side and touched her face. Kennedy's fingers barely brushed the area and came away sticky. *Blood.* She had to get this woman to the hospital.

More barking came from farther away. Someone yelled from outside the house, and then an engine roared. A door opened and shut.

Kennedy held her breath. Silence followed. She needed a weapon. After a check of the closet and finding no firearms, she swiped a big rubber mud boot. Anything was better than nothing.

"I'm going to get you help." She patted the woman's shoulder, even though Mrs. Barclay appeared unconscious—the sentiment more to calm her own nerves. As Kennedy stood, she heard movement outside the bedroom door.

Gripping the boot, she eased toward the entrance.

The door opened. "Liz…"

Kennedy swung with all her might, connecting with a man's jaw. Before she knew it, he'd grabbed her arm, stolen the boot, and thrown it behind him while holding her hand down by her side.

"Don't move." The man towered over her, and there was strength behind his grip.

She didn't listen. She kicked out, and her shoe connected with a leg.

"I'm not going to hurt you," he growled, and didn't release his hold. "Hold still. I'm a neighbor. The intruder is gone."

"A neighbor?" She stopped and looked up into his eyes—eye. A patch covered his left eye. Panic surged, and she kicked out again as she yanked her arm, trying to free herself.

He let her go, but remained in the doorway, blocking her escape.

She'd hoped to help Mrs. Barclay, but now Kennedy was the one in danger.

Texas Ranger Silas Boone couldn't make out the lady's features, but he knew to give a trapped animal distance. Right now, this woman needed room. His jaw stung from the slap.

"I'm Liz's neighbor, Silas Boone. I heard the dog barking and then thought I heard someone holler for help. I will not hurt you," he repeated.

The woman backed up, her hands grasping the wall, probably searching for the other boot.

His gaze landed on the body on the floor. *Liz.* His hand hit the light switch, but the room remained dark. He gulped a breath and raced to his neighbor's side. "What happened?" A touch to her neck indicated a weak pulse. "Have you called 9-1-1?"

"No." Suspicion laced her voice. "I dropped my phone."

"Who are you?" he snapped. "And what are you doing here?"

"My name is Kennedy Wells. I had an appointment with Mrs. Barclay."

He wasn't aware of a meeting but could ask more questions in a minute. Retrieving his cell phone from the holder on his belt, he called 9-1-1 and gave the dispatcher Liz's information and address.

He glanced Kennedy's way, but she had backed herself into a dark corner. "We need some light. I'll be right back."

Using the flashlight app on his cell phone, he found the electrical panel in the garage closet and flipped up the lever. Lights came on and appliances hummed to life.

When he returned to the room, the woman

was bending over his neighbor. "She's awfully pale. How long will it take for paramedics to get here?"

"Fifteen or twenty minutes."

"I pray that's soon enough. Are you certain that man is gone?" The woman finally looked up at him, their gazes connecting.

Silas stared. There was something familiar about her, but he couldn't identify it. The jeans and modest blue turtleneck showed an athletic build. His gaze went back to her face. Her eyes. That was it. He'd seen those brown eyes before. Her shoulder-length hair hung free, no doubt a little messed up from the skirmish. Suddenly, her brow furrowed, and he realized his staring made her uncomfortable.

His eye patch made folks nervous. Probably because people tried not to gawk but couldn't help themselves. At least she didn't look away like some did. What had she asked? "Yeah, the man fled. Are you injured?"

She shook her head.

Again, he recognized her sharp eyes. "Have we met before?"

"I don't think so."

Hmm. He was sure he'd seen that face before. "You said something about an appointment. Mind explaining who you are and why you're here?"

If his direct questions bothered her, she didn't show it. "Like I said, my name is Kennedy Wells. I had a seven-thirty appointment with Mrs. Barclay, but I was late. When I arrived, the lights were out and the front door open." She glanced around. "Where's dogzilla?"

Inwardly, he smiled at the accurate description. "I left Solomon outside. He'll warn us if the intruder returns."

Silas glanced around at the mess strewn on the floor. Drawers were open and the contents dumped. Elizabeth Barclay kept an immaculate house, and it appeared someone was looking for something. "You said you were here for an appointment?"

Kennedy nodded. "Yes. I noticed the front door wasn't closed when I knocked. I assumed she'd left it open so she'd hear me approach, but the dog was having a fit. When I stepped into the kitchen, I heard a crash. A man came into the room carrying a tire iron. After Solomon helped me get away, I ran back here and found her like this."

Silas glanced back at his longtime neighbor. Liz, as her friends called her, had been like a second mom to him and even babysat him when he was young. The gash on her head didn't appear deep, but there was a deep bluish bruise underneath. Concern ate at him that she hadn't regained consciousness.

The rural fire department was about fifteen minutes from their location, so when the sirens sounded in the distance, he was relieved the paramedics had responded quickly. He put Solomon in his crate in the garage so the first responders could do their job without being intimidated, and then went back into the bedroom.

Kennedy asked, "Did you know the man who attacked Mrs. Barclay?"

Silas was certain she tried to hide how the event had taken its toll, even though she wasn't able to stop her voice from shaking. "No, but I didn't get a good look at him. I only saw Solomon chase him around the house before a silver truck kicked up gravel. Did you know him?"

"Never seen him before. But with the house being dark, I might not have recognized him even if we had met before."

The lady seemed to be telling the truth. Who would attack Liz? His neighbor was one of the sweetest people he knew, and she certainly didn't deserve any more pain in her life. Wasn't losing a child and a husband anguish enough?

The paramedics arrived, and a minute later, a local police unit. Silas recognized the officer as Rex Trumble, a young officer fresh out of the academy. He had nothing against the kid, but he wished the department had sent a more experienced officer.

The paramedics, a man and woman, both in their forties, came through the door, and Silas showed them to the back room. After a quick check of Liz's vitals, they started an IV and loaded her onto a stretcher and into the waiting ambulance. Afterward, it only took fifteen minutes for Officer Trumble to take Kennedy's statement and check out the place. He didn't appear to write much down.

"Ma'am, it appears to be a simple burglary that you were unlucky enough to interrupt. Let me know if you recall any other details." Trumble nodded at Kennedy.

"I will." She gave the officer a half smile and released an audible breath.

While the first responders were tending to Liz, Silas considered the attack. Now that he had more time to scan the house, it didn't appear as if the intruder were there to steal. It looked more like the scene had been staged. Her small diamond ring was still on her finger. Even Liz's wallet, which had been discarded on the floor, still contained her credit cards and nineteen dollars in cash.

Something didn't add up.

Silas might be on medical leave from the Texas Rangers, but that didn't mean he had to ignore his neighbor's attack.

Kennedy turned those brown eyes on him. "I'm going to leave now. Thank you for your help." She paused. "I feel bad for all this happening to Mrs. Barclay. And I'm sorry I hit you with the boot."

He ignored the last comment but decided to gather more information. "You said you came here to interview her?" Liz's husband had passed away a couple of years ago. Even though she had two children who lived in the same county, he knew they were busy with their own lives. Silas had taken it upon himself to check on the widow ever since he'd gone on medical leave two months ago. "What was the interview about?"

She glanced at him like she was considering the request. "It was personal."

The color had returned to Kennedy's face, but he wasn't about to let it drop so easily. Liz took a blow to the head, and then the same person came after Kennedy. It might have been a simple case of theft, but Silas didn't believe that. "I care for Mrs. Barclay. A lot."

Kennedy continued to silently stare at him. "I'm a Texas Ranger."

More silence and staring. There it was again.

That feeling like he knew her. "I'm on medical leave." He pointed to his left eye. "Just until this heals."

"I need to go." She grabbed her backpack and threw the strap across her shoulder like she was about to leave but stopped. "My phone slid under the stove."

After she ran her hand along the edge but couldn't reach it, he went to the pantry and grabbed a broom. Using the stick end, he swept it out from under the appliance. The cell phone skittered to Kennedy's feet.

"Thanks." She picked it up and brushed away the dust. She looked at him and her shoulders slumped. "I'm a psychologist, Mr. Boone. The interview had nothing to do with the attack today."

He followed her out the door to her car. The lights on the ambulance swirled, lighting up the night sky and casting an eerie reflection on the trees. "I'm not trying to scare you, Miss Wells, but how do you know?"

Her head snapped up. "Know what?"

"That this had nothing to do with your interview. I don't believe this was a break-in or a theft. Nothing important was taken. The intruder used a tire iron. Not exactly your weapon of choice for stealing from a stranger."

Her straightforward gaze stayed connected with his as she listened intently.

"What did the man have to gain by attacking you? He should've run off if all he wanted to do was get away. Yet he tried to take you out."

"Maybe he thought I could identify him."

"Could be. He didn't even take Liz's credit cards or cash." He cocked his head at her.

"That *is* strange." She sighed and tossed her backpack into the passenger seat. "To put your mind at ease, I've never even met Mrs. Barclay. I work as a psychologist at a local counseling center, and I also volunteer with Bring the Children Home Project—an organization that helps find missing children. Harper Barclay's case came across my desk. Mrs. Barclay was gracious enough to agree to discuss her daughter's abduction."

If Kennedy had punched Silas in the gut, it wouldn't have surprised him more.

Harper Barclay. His life changed forever the day she was kidnapped. No matter how many times he tried to forget, memories of watching three-year-old Harper being abducted from the park plagued his consciousness.

Although he had been nine, he felt that if he'd been faster, he could've stopped the woman from throwing his young neighbor into that van. Watching helplessly as she was abducted made him want to protect the innocent, and later, made him get into law enforcement.

The memory of Harper screaming his name occasionally still woke him at night.

Silas jerked as he looked at Kennedy again. The heart-shaped face, button nose and lips that were pressed into a thin line at the moment. But it was the expressive brown eyes that demanded his attention. They were identical to Harper Barclay's age-progression photo.

That was impossible.

"What? Why are you looking at me like that?" She frowned. "Did I say something wrong?"

The chances of Harper being alive were slim to none, but he continued to look at her files every year or two when there became a lull in his cases. "No. You said nothing wrong."

Did Kennedy have any idea she looked identical to the missing girl?

If she were Harper Barclay, whoever kidnapped her would not want the truth to come out.

That put Kennedy in grave danger.

TWO

The look on the Texas Ranger's face grew solemn, urging Kennedy to cut their conversation short.

He cocked his head, his uncovered eye staring at her. "Is there another reason you're the one who got picked to interview Mrs. Barclay?"

Another reason? What did that mean? She gave him a slight smile, trying to mask her frustration. "Look, I don't know why all the questions. I've never met Elizabeth Barclay before today. I was picked because I work for the missing children's team and am one member who performs the intake." Her tone was dismissive. "I need to get home."

Bliss Walker, the creator and leader of the team, insisted everyone in the group be up for the emotional task of helping these families. Kennedy was one of the three members who did intakes. She interviewed the families, filled out their information and brought it back to the group. Kennedy's primary job, however, was to offer specialized therapy and counseling for the grief of having a family member go missing. She also had a list of counselors in all parts of the state she could recommend if the family were too far away from north Texas for her to counsel personally.

Even though Bring the Children Home Project tried to help everyone, Bliss had the final say of what cases to accept. Being as this was a cold case and there were no other local children missing at the moment, Kennedy believed her boss would take this one. Liberty was a rural farming community, so there weren't many abduction cases in the small north Texas town. It would help if there were new clues or information where they could look into the case again. That was one question she had intended to ask Elizabeth Barclay.

"The ambulance is ready to leave." Silas turned to walk away but stopped and looked at her. "Would you like me to see you home?"

"No, I'll be fine." Kennedy didn't believe the attacker had been after her. Surely, she'd just been at the wrong place at the wrong time.

Silas scrutinized her like he wanted to argue. Like he was debating saying something. "Are you certain?"

"Of course."

He finally reached into the back pocket of his jeans and pulled out a business card. "Call me if you need anything. I'm going to follow the ambulance to the hospital. I'd like to talk with you more if that's all right, maybe in the morning."

"I won't need anything. But thanks." Before he could say anything more, she shut her car door, turned the vehicle around and waited for the ambulance to pull out. They were several miles from the main highway, and she didn't want to impede their route.

After the Texas Ranger's 4x4 truck exited the drive, she followed at a distance. What was wrong with that guy? The way he stared at her was unnerving. He was handsome as all get-out, even with the patch over his eye. Kind of gave him that pirate, bad-boy look—something she wasn't interested in, but still… Officer Trumble had given her the number to the station if she needed help. Even Mr. Boone admitted he was on medical leave.

Maybe Silas was finding it difficult to keep busy while off work. *That* she could understand. Last year, she'd taken seven weeks off to help care for her terminally ill mother. What Kennedy didn't comprehend was why the Ranger kept giving her that strange look.

As she drove across the county to her home thirty-five minutes away, she thought about the attack. Silas was right that it made little sense the man came after her. He didn't appear to have taken anything. Maybe he had mistakenly believed he'd killed Mrs. Barclay and would be accused of murder and Kennedy would be the only witness.

Chills marched down the back of her neck.

At least he didn't know Kennedy's name or address. He hadn't stolen her purse or anything that gave away her identity. That was a relief.

As she reached to turn on the radio, her gaze went to the long scratch on her arm. So close to getting hurt. If it hadn't been for the humongous dog, she might not have gotten away.

Thick trees made an eerie tunnel of the road. Only the beams of her headlights broke through the blackness. Suddenly, bright lights shone in her rearview mirror like someone had pulled out from a side road. The high beams blinded her. She switched the mirror to night setting and decelerated. When that didn't help, she pulled to the side of the road so the vehicle could pass. As it approached, the huge automobile picked up speed and veered toward her.

What are they doing?

Her heart leaped in her chest, and she hit the gas. Too late. The truck rammed her bumper, making her head smack into the headrest and sent her Mini Cooper careening toward the ditch. She screamed.

Oh please, God, help me.

With a jolt, her car slammed into the side of the trench and ran over several saplings—the branches running up the hood and disappearing over the windshield. Screeching limbs, along with the revving of an engine, filled the air.

She jerked the steering wheel and kept her foot pressed on the gas. With her wheels spinning, the car bumped along the steep ditch, finally regaining traction, and she got back on the road, going sideways. She brought the car under control. Thirty miles per hour. Forty. Fifty. The truck remained on her tail as her speed climbed higher. She had to get away from this guy.

Silas.

She grabbed her phone from the console without taking her eyes off the road. Maybe she could reach him before he got too far ahead. What did she do with his business card? It was in her passenger seat. As she reached for the card, her front driver's side tire hit a pothole and sent her phone flying into the floorboard. There was no way she could reach it without wrecking.

Bam.

The truck rammed her again. Her head bashed into the side window and lights flashed before her eyes. He was going to kill her if she didn't get off this road. His front bumper locked with the back of her car and spun her out of control. She tried to hang on, but it was no use. Her car whipped toward the left, off the road, and slammed into a tree.

Ignoring the throbbing pain, she opened the door and started to run for the woods, but with her headlight plastered against the tree trunk, darkness swallowed her sight. The ditch dipped sharply, causing her to fall to one knee.

Tires slid on gravel. A door slammed. He was coming.

She scrambled back to her feet and saw a barbwire fence just in time. Spikes stabbed her thigh, but she couldn't worry about a few cuts. She crossed through the sagging strands and dashed for the safety of the dense trees. Vines and shrubs tore at her jeans.

Heavy breathing came from behind her.

He was gaining on her.

She should've taken Silas up on his offer to see her home.

Kennedy's low-heel dress boot came down on a fallen branch and her foot twisted. Even as pain shot up her leg, she couldn't stop.

She had to hide!

How far away was the closest house? Mrs. Barclay's place was a few miles away.

A large cedar tree loomed in front of her. Crouching down, she slid underneath the lower branches. Her lungs begged for air, but she attempted to control the heavy panting so he couldn't hear.

Crash. Then pounding footsteps hurried past her about ten yards away.

She waited until the sounds grew quieter before crawling from underneath the heavy branch. Mrs. Barclay's place was to the east, and she'd have to cross the road somewhere along the path. It was essential she get far enough away so the man wouldn't be able to see her. Maybe he'd give up and go back to his truck.

The trees were so thick virtually no moonlight shone through. She continued in a northeast direction, hoping the guy continued straight north and that he'd give up his search.

After several minutes, a hum echoed in the distance. She stopped and listened but couldn't identify the source. Another hundred yards, and she recognized the sound of running water.

Was that the Red River?

She hadn't realized she'd gone that far. There weren't many bridges that passed over the river into Oklahoma. Fearing there'd be no way to cross, she headed directly east. How long would it take her to get back to Mrs. Barclay's place? At least she'd have a place to wait until daylight. Solomon could protect her.

Or maybe the gigantic dog wouldn't recognize her, and he'd attack. Great.

A light breeze blew, causing the cold of night to cut straight through her turtleneck. She was hot-natured and hadn't worn a jacket.

The trees thinned, and an open field of harvested wheat lay in front of her. She'd be in the open if she continued into the field. And she couldn't go back. The way the man had gone was a shorter route, but she kept to the edge of the trees instead.

Her legs burned, and her ankle ached. The boot grew tight, telling her swelling had set in. How could she have been so thoughtless not to allow Silas to follow her home? She simply couldn't fathom that the man who attacked Mrs. Barclay would come after her.

No one would notice if she didn't come home tonight. No one would miss her until Sunday morning when she didn't show up at church.

Her dad had been struggling since her mother's death thirteen months earlier. Kennedy didn't want to admit it, but she was afraid he was showing signs of dementia. Dad only lived a mile from her, and he had plans to go fishing early in the morning. Stone River Counseling was closed until Monday for renovations, so they weren't expecting her to come to work. Over thirty-six hours before anyone would notice she was missing. The thought was terrifying and depressing.

Sounds of flowing water continued as she wound her way through the brush.

Suddenly, a branch snapped.

She stopped mid-step and listened. Silence. Hopefully, a squirrel or rabbit. Or even a wild pig or coyote would be better than a madman intent on killing her.

About the time she concluded it was nothing, another *crunch* from the trees. She bristled. A glance over her shoulder, and all she saw was the desolate woods, nothing but dark shadows forming a black wall that rose until it melded into the night sky.

Something moved that was too tall to be an animal. Her heart drummed in her ears.

Someone was watching her.

Had the man come up behind her? Chill bumps broke out on her arms. Mrs. Barclay's place was at least a mile away. There was no way she could make it without getting caught.

She took a timid step back. And then another. Finally, she turned and ran. She sprinted over brush and dodged trees. Limbs slapped her face as she shoved them aside with her arm and ran for her life.

Her heart rate picked up. Even as she bolted, she looked around for a rock or stick to use as a weapon. She wouldn't go down without a fight.

Suddenly, a culvert appeared in front of her. An old, partly crushed tin horn overgrown with dead johnsongrass led into an adjoining pasture.

A shot rang out and something whizzed past her.

Dressed in running shoes, she might have a chance, but not in these stupid boots. She glanced again at the tin horn. Her limbs shook with panic. She hated confined places.

Could she fit in there?

Dropping to her knees, she stuck her head into the opening. *You can do this*. Holding back a scream, she moved one knee forward. Her breath was sucked from her lungs and dizziness made her head swim.

Please, God, help me do this!

Don't think about it, she admonished herself. Drawing a deep breath, she inched forward and ducked even lower, her shoulders brushing against the sides of the contraption.

Her mouth went dry like cotton was packed in her throat, making it impossible to swallow.

She couldn't do it. She couldn't make herself move another inch.

Footsteps moved in the tall grass.

Oh no. He was coming.

One. Two. Three. Closing her eyes, she refused to think about what would happen if she got stuck in the tight space and continued to worm her way into the culvert. Sweat drenched her body.

Could he see her shoes? Silently, she bent her knees as much as the space would allow until her boots were past the entrance.

The footsteps stopped.

She held her breath, even as her heart threatened to explode. There was no escape if he found her. She was all alone. No one would come looking for her.

Oh, please, God. I need help.

Silas checked his phone again. Kennedy still hadn't called him back.

He turned down Old Carpenter's Bluff Road toward Liz Barclay's. Blessed with a superb memory, he'd remembered the number and address Kennedy had given to Officer Trumble. After he'd arrived at the hospital, Silas worried about her, kicking himself for not insisting on following her home. He'd called his friend, Texas Ranger Randolph, and had him check out Kennedy's home. She still hadn't arrived back there, and he'd left Liz's over two hours ago.

His headlights reflected off a car on the side of the road. As he approached, his heart sank. Kennedy's red Mini Cooper sat in the ditch with the back bumper demolished and back window busted out.

He jumped out of the truck and glanced in the driver's-side door, but the car was empty. Two sets of deep tire ruts scarred the rocky road, telling him another vehicle had been here. Grabbing a flashlight from his console, he pointed it at the ground by the driver's-side door. The grass was beaten down toward the barbwire fence.

Dense woods lay in front of him, and the Red River ran parallel to the road a half mile behind him. Considering her car was on the same side of the woods as the trampled grass, he assumed she ran that way.

The property had been a deer lease for many years and the woods were expansive. He'd never get his truck through there. Since he was only a few miles from his ranch, he jumped back in his truck and headed that way.

Minutes later, he came to a screeching stop

in front of his equipment shed and climbed on his ATV. He knew the well-used trail to the woods like the back of his hand and kept an eye out for movement and lights.

Was Kennedy even out here?

Those brown eyes captivated his mind. If she were Harper, did she understand the danger that put her in? He needed to tell her his suspicions.

Twenty minutes had passed as he weaved his way across dry creek beds and through the trees. Small saplings and broken branches littered the narrow trail, but his ATV crashed through. He came to a clearing and killed the engine.

After listening and hearing nothing but the typical night sounds of coyotes and a hoot owl somewhere, he called Kennedy's name.

No answer.

He started the ATV, and not knowing what direction she would've gone, took off again at a slower speed. Ranger Randolph agreed to wait at Kennedy's house and let him know if she arrived home. It was possible she might not have gone home but had a family member pick her up after she wrecked her car.

His instinct, though, told him she was out here somewhere.

A structure stuck out above the treetops. A

deer stand. The thing had been out here ever since Silas was a kid. Even though the wood showed signs of rot, he carefully climbed the ladder and peered inside. Only an old bird's nest, leaves and rodent droppings.

As he got back on the trail, his lights reflected from a pair of taillights.

When he drew closer, he realized it was a pickup. A quick glance confirmed it was the same truck as the intruder's vehicle that sped away from Liz's place. An open box of shotgun shells sat in the front seat.

A tight ball formed in Silas's stomach. Which direction would Kennedy have gone? And even more important, where was the guy who presumably carried the shotgun?

One minute later, he was back on the trail. Where to? He tried to put himself into Kennedy's place to figure out which way she would've gone. Assuming she had no weapon, he thought she would stick to the protection of the woods. But he doubted if she knew her way around these parts.

Back to the Barclays'? It's the only place that made sense. An opening in the trees on the road appeared in front of him to the left. That way led to the river. There'd be no escape. Surely she hadn't gone that way unless she didn't realize where the path led. Silas turned down the road while keeping a lookout for their attacker.

After a few minutes, the land topped out on a hill where he could see better. He pulled off the trail, killed the engine and made sure his gun was secured in the holster before climbing off the machine. He wound his way silently through the trees. Fifty yards ahead, he detected a dark shadow moving. The limbs and brush made it impossible to tell if the figure was a man or woman.

He watched for a moment but didn't see the person anymore. Taking a wide swath to the right, he moved closer, careful to keep watch. If Kennedy was nearby, then Silas didn't want her to be in his line of fire in case he shot at the shadow. As he neared, reflection from what appeared to be a gun glistened in the moonlight. A shotgun came into view, and it was pointed at something in the clearing.

Every muscle in Silas's body tensed. In one smooth motion, he removed his Glock from the holster and pointed. He'd practiced shooting since his eye injury, but his aim was still a tad off. He couldn't afford mistakes.

With his arm outstretched, Silas took aim. *Boom.*

Deafening silence followed the discharging of the shotgun.

Silas held his fire. Tension gripped him, stunned that the man from the pickup truck had pulled the trigger before he could react. A slight chill traveled down the back of his neck as his gaze franticly sought out Kennedy.

Where was she?

Please, Lord, don't have let me be too late to save her.

THREE

A gunshot reverberated through the tin horn. Kennedy let out a small squeal. She berated herself for the noisy response. Hopefully the shooter hadn't heard.

The blood beating in her ears was thunderous. Where was the shooter?

Maybe she should run for it.

She inched forward to the middle of the tin horn. A jagged piece of metal tugged at her hair. Rocks bit into her hands and knees. She pushed the terror to the back of her mind. Thoughts of snakes or getting trapped in this thing couldn't take over her brain. If they did, she'd panic, and he'd catch her for sure.

While concentrating on controlling her breathing, her shoulder cramped at the awkward position, and she tried to twist her body enough to relieve the tension. It was no use. The space was too confined. No sounds or movements came from outside. Where had her pursuer gone? Had he seen her, or just fired his gun in hopes she'd run and give away her position?

She waited for what seemed like forever. A glance at the end of the tin horn showed nothing except for the silhouette of dead grass blowing in the breeze.

How long had she been out here? She'd left Mrs. Barclay's place a little after nine o'clock. It must be somewhere close to eleven or after. Coyotes howled in the distance. That was good, right? Didn't animals grow silent when people were moving around? Or maybe that was just in the movies.

Her head dropped to her shoulder, and her eyes shut. The effort not to panic became a little easier as long as she locked the claustrophobic thoughts in the back of her mind. One thought of getting stuck or not being able to breathe, and she could hyperventilate. In the morning, she would crawl out and walk back to Barclay's or some neighbor's place. Surely the gunman would be gone by then.

Sometime later, there was movement outside her metal prison. She glanced out the end of the tin horn but saw nothing but darkness.

Something moved in the grass close by.

Oh no. Had he figured out where she was? Should she run?

Yes. She couldn't just sit here. As quietly as possible, she inched forward. If the animal or person outside was still on the move, she couldn't hear it. When she was almost at the end of the tunnel, her palm came down on a plastic lid, creating a loud *crack*.

She froze.

Footsteps moved closer. She couldn't be a sitting duck.

Again, she crawled forward. This end of the tin horn was crushed, and she hoped she could fit. Worming her way through, painstakingly slow, she finally made it to the opening. She glanced around, wishing there were more moonlight. Tall grass lined the narrow ditch and the dark silhouette of a bare pecan tree loomed in the distance.

This might be her only chance. She had to take it.

She ducked her head and pressed against the rusty tin until it gave way enough for her head to push through. As she continued her progress, her shoulders caught, making her heart stampede. She was almost free. *Breathe. Breathe.* She counted. *One. Two. Three.* She pushed with all her might, and the tin broke away, causing her to fall forward. Chilly air blew her hair. Freedom at last.

Suddenly, a powerful hand covered her mouth.

She attempted to scream, but the hand was too strong.

"Be quiet. Or he'll hear you."

Intent on freeing herself, she continued to fight for survival. Air. She needed air.

"It's me, Silas," he whispered. "I need to get you out of here."

She blinked. Silas? How had he found her or even known she was missing? He helped her out and put his fingers to his lips, signaling her to remain quiet.

Keeping low, he led her into the trees along the path she'd taken earlier. Once they had gone twenty yards, she tugged on his arm. "The gunman is this way. We need to go back."

He squatted on his haunches as he looked around. "I saw him move on, probably back to his truck parked in the woods. The guy shot his shotgun I'd guess hoping to scare you out into the open."

"I heard that! Scared me to death. I thought he saw me."

"Nope. I'd taken aim at him and was afraid I was too late. After he fired, I didn't want to take a shot not knowing your location. He waited a good thirty minutes in this area, so I figure he knows you were nearby. I have my ATV a half mile back in the trees. Come on. Let's get to it."

She followed closely. She hadn't heard an ATV, or even the gunman's truck. Relief that Silas had returned impressed her. The clouds moved over the moon, making it difficult to see, so she kept her hand on his back. For a big man, he moved quietly.

Kennedy tried not to think about how she'd gotten into this mess. Had the gunman simply targeted her because she was a witness to Mrs. Barclay's attack and could identify him? But try as she might, questions continued to plague her mind.

Silas had asked if the interview had made her a target. But why? Who would know she was asking questions about a twenty-six-year-old cold case? She'd told Bliss Walker, the CEO of Bring the Children Home Project, about the interview with Elizabeth Barclay. Maybe her boss told someone about the meeting. But Bliss was discreet and wasn't one to talk up a case.

Again, who would care if a kidnapping cold case were being investigated?

The kidnapper would. How would someone know she was meeting Mrs. Barclay?

The trail dipped into a shallow creek, and Kennedy almost lost her balance, causing her to run into Silas's back.

He turned, keeping his voice down. "You all right?"

"I'm fine." Her ankle ached, but it was minor.

He searched her eyes, the intenseness unnerving, before he started walking again.

She swallowed. What was it about him that caused her heart to stutter? Sure, he was nice-looking, but he wasn't the only man she'd ever met who fell into the handsome category. Maybe it was the way he looked at her, like he was searching for something. Scrutinizing her. Normally she was good at reading people, but not so with the Texas Ranger.

As they topped the rise, an ATV came into view.

After a trek down the slight hill, they climbed on the ATV, Kennedy seated behind him. Her seat mainly consisted of the metal rack—a hard, uncomfortable place to sit, but at least it was sturdy.

As they took off, she held on to the rack. The road was full of potholes and littered with roots and forest debris. Her body shuddered with each hit, and her hands clenched the sides of the metal rods on each side of her.

A shot split the night, making her jump. Her grip tightened. A limb above them fell into the path they drove on, and the ATV ran up and over it with a jolt. Did the gunman really want to kill them both? Why?

"Hang on."

Kennedy held on to the rack tighter.

They made their way through the woods to the north, to where the trees thinned. The trail was still rough, but at least it was straight. Somewhere to the left, headlights shone through the trees. The man was still coming their way. How did he make it through the woods in the truck? There wasn't room on the trails. He must've known a back way and be familiar with the place.

After a couple of minutes, they came to a long wooden bridge. A heavy iron frame towered above, and Silas stopped.

"What are you doing?" she squeaked. "We don't have time to stop. The guy is coming."

"We can't cross here." He put the ATV in Reverse and started backing up to turn around.

Headlights bore down on them, and the truck's engine roared. The driver was going to ram them.

"Go. Go."

A concrete pole stood in the middle of the road, supposedly to create a barrier for people not to enter, but Silas swung the ATV around the barricade and onto the rickety bridge.

Kennedy didn't understand the problem of crossing the bridge, but she could sense Silas was looking for another way. If they could get to the other side, surely, they could lose this guy. The crossing looked too narrow for the truck.

The farther they went, the more the rotted boards sagged and bowed. She wrapped her arms tighter around his waist and closed her eyes. *Please, please, God, help us make it across.*

The ATV rocked with the movements and twice she felt it dip. When she opened her eyes, their headlights reflected off water. They were much higher than she anticipated. She turned to see if the man had followed, but he'd stopped at the entrance.

Silas slowed the ATV.

"What's wrong?"

She leaned over to look around him. At least three boards were missing. They couldn't do this. They'd have to turn around!

A shot blasted through the air, and something whizzed past her ear.

"Keep your head down and hang on tight." Silas backed up a few feet and then floored it.

"We can't jump this!" Every muscle in her body tensed as they flew across the decaying bridge and across the gap. The back tires landed half off the board.

"Lean forward!"

She pushed as hard as she could into his back. He continued holding down the gas and the back tires spun. The smell of rubber filled the air.

There was another gun blast.

Finally, the tires found traction and again were on solid boards. They took off.

Sparks flew as a pellet hit the back of the ATV.

She turned. The man was out of his truck and on the bridge. He was coming toward them with his shotgun pointed. "Hurry!"

The guy fired another shot.

The ATV went sharply to the right, slammed into the railing, and rode up the edge. The machine tilted sideways, threatening to flip. Kennedy had never been so petrified in her life.

As the ATV's side tires continued along the metal rails, the machine propelled along like it had a mind of its own. Kennedy squeezed her eyes shut and wrapped her arms around the cowboy's waist, preparing to plummet into the river.

Pellets zipped past as Silas fought to get the ATV off the decrepit bridge framework, but the front tire got caught in the groove like a roller coaster at a theme park, out of control. Suddenly, the metal rail ended, and the front end of the ATV dropped to the crumbling wooden platform, jarring them from the move.

Up ahead, several boards were missing. Silas gassed it, hoping to jump it again.

A board broke under his front left tire, making him lose control. And then another board. A pellet smashed into the handlebar. Realizing he couldn't hurdle the space, he hit the brakes.

But it was too late. The front end pitched forward, the front tires ran out of boards, and then they were falling.

Kennedy's scream reverberated in his ears.

The Red River swallowed them. For a second, the impact and the cold left him dazed, the slow current tugging him under. Being free from the ATV, he kicked his feet and broke the water's surface.

Where was Kennedy?

His boots weighed him down as he searched for her in the moonlight, the eye patch making it difficult to see. At least the water wasn't deep, barely over their heads. About ten feet away, he saw a hand and water splash. He dove for her and caught her arm, tugging her above water.

She gasped and spit water.

Silas put himself between Kennedy and the shooter. Movement caught his attention as the man strode across the bridge toward them. Silas whispered, "Come on. Stay low, the shooter is still there."

"You've…got to be kidding me." Her words mixed with pants for air, and her voice trembled, probably from the freezing water. "Can we cross to other side?"

He continued to glance back at the bridge as they swam farther downriver. "Too far." The man raised the shotgun again. "Get down."

Boom.

Kennedy gulped water as Silas tugged her under. Even as they went beneath the surface, he continued towing them downstream. When he felt her fighting, he hauled her up again. She gagged on the water.

"Sorry. We need to get away from this guy." His gaze searched the bridge. Nothing. He'd lost sight of the man.

Headlight beams hit the top of the treetops on the Texas side of the river as a vehicle approached.

"Is that him?" Kennedy asked breathlessly.

"I don't know. If so, he didn't turn on his lights when he took off because his truck was parked over there." Silas pointed to indicate the foot of the bridge and continued to watch as he started for the bank. The water was shallow here, only knee-level, but he made a beeline for the area overgrown in the brush. The shadows of the trees should hide them from the moonlight, making it difficult to spot them. He climbed up the three-foot red-sand bank and held out his hand. She took it, and he hauled her up.

"I don't see the gunman." Kennedy's gaze went to the bridge as she shivered and wrapped her arms around herself. "Do you think he's headed this way?"

"I don't know." He continued to watch the headlights as a pickup stopped a few feet from the bridge. Did the gunman have an accomplice? Maybe he called someone to pick him up. But as they both remained still, the engine died, and someone got out of the vehicle. A door slammed. "Silas, are you out here?"

Silas glanced heavenward and let out a pent-up breath. "I am."

"I suppose you know whoever that is?" Kennedy raised her eyebrows.

"Yeah. That's Texas Ranger Randolph, who I had watching your house. I'm glad he decided to check on me." He took her hand and started winding their way up the bank toward the road. At her questioning gaze, he explained. "After I left for the hospital to see Liz, I was worried about you and wanted to be certain you made it home."

Her free hand went to her throat, and her voice was incredulous. "You did? I don't understand what's going on. I guess it's because I'm a witness to Mrs. Barclay's attack."

Silas stopped and looked at her. Should he tell her his suspicions? What if he was wrong? She deserved to know the possibilities. "Kennedy, have you looked at Harper Barclay's case?"

"Of course, I have. She was an adorable little girl. It's a very sad story, like most of our cases."

The longer he stared at Kennedy's brown eyes, the more he was convinced she was Harper. "I've been neighbors with the Barclays for over thirty years. No one has ever attacked Liz or broken into her home until now. You may be right that this was a random break-in, and you happened to be at the wrong place at the wrong time. But I don't think so."

She blinked, and her face turned ashen. "What are you trying to say?"

"Have you seen Harper's age-progression photo?"

"No, I just received the file two days ago."

"I'd like for you to come by my house and look at my laptop. I believe *you* are Harper Barclay." At her incredulous look, he kept talking. "The Texas Rangers have an exceptional age-progression specialist. You need to see the photo. You'll be looking in a mirror."

"You're kidding me." Kennedy laughed out

loud before sobering. She tilted her head to the side and pursed her lips in thought. Finally, she shrugged. "I'll do it. I just hate to disappoint you when you see I'm not Harper. I have a dad, and my mom died just over a year ago. They were the best parents a girl could ask for—and I can guarantee you, they did not kidnap me."

He hoped she was right. But deep in his gut, he knew she was wrong.

Silas could see Ranger Randolph pacing beside his truck as they came out of the trees near the bridge. One thing was certain, if she were Harper Barclay, whoever kidnapped her would not want her looking into the case and was prepared to stop at nothing—including murder.

FOUR

Kennedy sat in the warm cab of Ranger Randolph's truck and watched the two Texas Rangers chat with each other. Her knees trembled slightly from racing for her life and from being cold and wet. It was almost like she was watching a movie, looking in but not being a part of the script.

But that wasn't true at all. Her clothes were soaked, adding to the misery. Cuts and bruises covered her arms and legs from running through the woods. Her ankle hurt. The sound of water flowing reached her ears. But most of all, a man named Silas Boone was in the flesh and standing in view.

This was terrifyingly real.

She had to get a hold of herself. No, she might not normally put herself in danger like her team members, but she'd heard the stories. Talked to her clients. Kind of like the scripture that talked about if the man had known when the thief would come, the homeowner would watch and not let his house be broken into. Kennedy knew bad things happened to people every day, counseled them, she just didn't think danger would happen to her. The most logical conclusion of this whole incident was the guy believed he'd killed Mrs. Barclay and had come after Kennedy because he thought she was a witness.

"...back to my house." Silas's voice carried to her.

"You want me to call the lieutenant?"

Silas put his hand in the air. "I know." He glanced over his shoulder at her, and then his voice dropped too low to hear.

No doubt he was telling Ranger Randolph his idea that *she* was Harper Barclay. The thought was surreal and laughable. If Silas had only known her mom, he never would've thought such a thing.

Silas walked her way, and she rolled down her window. "Are you ready to go? Randolph can drop us off at my house where I can get my truck."

Did she have a choice without her car? "Sure. I'd like to get my car if it's drivable."

He nodded. "Sure."

"Where are your manners, Boone? You didn't introduce us before shoving her into the cab of my truck." The cowboy with the lanky build strode to her, a smile on his face. He stuck his hand out. "I'm Texas Ranger Randolph."

She shook his hand in greeting. Being that she was dripping wet like a drowned rat, the action seemed too formal. "Kennedy Wells."

"Glad to meet you. Don't let this guy scare you none." With a jerk of his head, he indicated Silas. "He acts all tough, but he's really a big softy."

"Okay, Randolph. The lady has had a rough night." Silas put himself between her and the other Ranger. "Let's go."

Kennedy opened the door. "Let me get in the back."

Silas held up his hand. "Stay up front where it's warmer."

She was pretty certain the heat also blew in the back, and Silas was also wet, but she didn't argue. Truth was, even with the heat, she was still freezing. Both Rangers climbed in, Silas behind her seat.

"I'll make certain she makes it home safely tonight," Silas said.

"Okay. Let me know if you need anything. Oh…" Randolph grabbed a business card from the console and handed it to her. "If you need to reach me."

"Thanks." These guys must have boxes of cards to hand out. Since her pockets were wet, she held the card in her hand. Maybe she would wake in the morning to find everything had been a bad dream. She shivered even with the heat blowing on full blast.

"They're not fashionable, but I have some sweats at my house if you want to change into dry clothes."

She looked at Ranger Randolph. "Could we stop by my car and see if it's drivable? If not, I have some clothes in the trunk." They were workout clothes, but she wasn't picky at the moment.

"Sure." The cowboy glanced in the rearview mirror, evidently making sure that was all right with Silas. The other Ranger didn't say a word, so she assumed they had his approval.

A few minutes later, Randolph parked on the side of the road next to her car.

Silas opened the door. "I'll try to get your car out of the ditch and check to see if it's drivable."

Kennedy got out with him and stayed on the road while he went into the tall grass. She'd left the keys in the ignition, and he gave it a try. The car fired right up, but when he put it in Reverse, it barely moved. He tried rocking it out, and gassed it, but the car scarcely budged.

"It's not going anywhere tonight. Here's your phone."

"Thanks. Looks like I have no choice but to wait until tomorrow." She retrieved the keys and phone from Silas. After rifling through her trunk, she found her yoga pants and sweatshirt. "I got what I need."

They got back in the truck and several minutes later, Randolph pulled into what she assumed was Silas's drive. Mrs. Barclay's house sat next door, and the trees were so thick the house couldn't be seen if it weren't for a security light illuminating the woman's car.

She got out of the truck and shivered as the men mumbled some last words to each other. Randolph turned the truck around and exited the drive, leaving them standing in darkness.

"I'd like to get changed and go home, please."

Silas looked at her. "Won't you at least look at the progression images? I know it's been a long night, but I think you should know what Harper Barclay looks like today."

The pleading in his voice moved her, but she didn't like it. What if he was right, and she looked identical to Harper? What then? Did she even want to know? Couldn't she go on about her life and pretend none of this ever happened? Even as the thought crossed her mind, she reprimanded herself for being a chicken.

She wasn't Harper. There was nothing to fear. Besides, she often counseled clients to stand back and look at the big picture. If one could do so, the immediate future didn't seem as overwhelming or powerful. It was easier to give advice than to take it. Her mom used to tell her she wasn't good at asking for help. Maybe it was true. Keeping the focus on the other person meant you didn't have to fix yourself.

Silas must've misinterpreted her silence. He sighed. "Come on. I'll take you home." He strode for the vehicle parked outside a metal shed.

"I'll go in."

He turned around. "Are you certain?"

"I'll never be able to relax once I get home if I don't." She followed him up the stone steps to his ranch-style house, complete with cedar siding and massive windows.

He flipped on the light, exposing the stone floor and high ceilings. "First, let's get you a towel." He disappeared down a hall and returned with two towels—those huge body-sized ones that covered you head to toe—and handed one to her. "The bathroom is the second door on your right. There are plastic bags under the sink if you need something to put your wet clothes in."

"Thank you." She hurried down the hall to get changed. It only took a couple of minutes to get into the dry clothes and scrub her hair dry. She found a comb in the drawer and ran it through her hair and then fluffed it with her fingers. One glance at her reflection and she realized this was no time to look in a mirror.

When she returned, the living room was empty. Footsteps sounded behind, and she turned to see Silas striding toward her carrying a pair of boots and clad in a pair of jeans and a black Western shirt that was left untucked. He sat on the couch and pulled on his cowboy boots. She'd be willing to guess he owned several pairs.

He glanced up and stood. "Let me power up my laptop. I could use my phone, but I'd rather have a larger image."

The smell of leather greeted her, and the massive fireplace with a simple cedar mantel drew the eye to the focal point of the room.

"Is this your house?"

"I guess you could say that. I had it built for my grandma a few years back. My grandparents' large farmhouse wasn't equipped for wheelchairs and had electrical and plumbing issues, not to mention hard to heat and cool.

When my granddad passed away, I built this for my grandma. Only two bedrooms and easier to take care of."

"That was nice of you."

"Family is important."

She glanced back to him before turning her attention to his computer that sat on the coffee table in front of a leather couch, and not on a desk. Not wanting to appear to be snooping, her feet stayed planted in one place. A row of what she assumed was the Ranger's family photos rested on the mantel. A couple in black and white showed an elderly people standing in front of an old car and a barn in the background. Was that the same barn that was outside? Probably, but she hadn't gotten a good look at it. Several more photos showed a younger version of Silas with a couple and a girl. She supposed his little sister and parents.

A glance out the window showed the cedars swayed in the wind at the Barclay place. They were majestic, tall and in nice, straight rows. "The trees next door almost look like they were planted."

He glanced up and stared at her. "They were planted. The Barclays used to own a Christmas tree farm." He looked over her shoulder and pointed. "Tents were set up over there, and they'd serve hot chocolate or cider to their customers."

That sounded lovely. Kennedy had always wanted to visit a tree farm for Christmas, but her parents always used a small artificial tree because her mom was allergic to cedar.

"Come on. I have the picture pulled up."

Drawing a deep breath, she crossed the room and took a seat on the couch. Silas turned the laptop to face her.

A flash of adrenaline tingled throughout her body, causing her stomach to flutter. Silas was right. She was looking at a mirror image.

Her mouth went dry, and she could feel Silas's gaze on her. "I don't know what to say. Except for the hairstyle, this *does* look like me."

"I know," he whispered. He held a finger in the air. "I'll be right back." He disappeared down a hall, leaving her alone to gawk at the screen.

But what now? Even though she admitted she looked like Harper, it didn't mean she *was* Harper.

She glanced back at the screen. In the bottom corner was a Texas Ranger file number. Was the man obsessed or something? He'd gone above and beyond to find the little girl.

He returned with his shirt tucked in.

"Why are you so interested in this case?"

He stared down at his boots for a moment before turning his attention back to her. "I witnessed Harper being taken at the park. I was in charge of her."

"What do you mean in charge? Surely you're not that much older."

"Liz was my babysitter and asked me to keep an eye on Harper while she took another child to the restroom."

Several silent seconds ticked by. The only sound was that of an antique clock on the mantel. Silas witnessed the kidnapping. Nausea swirled in her belly. She needed to talk to her dad. "I'd like to go home now."

Silas knew Kennedy was struggling with the news, but he was more concerned about her safety. He knew nothing about her since the day she was taken. If she was the one who'd been abducted, who took her? Her parents? "Does anyone live in the home with you?"

"No." She shook her head. "Maybe I should call my dad to come pick me up."

"I don't mind taking you home. It's late. I can get a tow strap from my shop and pull your car out in the morning."

She offered a frustrated smile. "Thanks. I hate to put you out more than I already have."

"I don't mind. I'm on medical leave, anyway.

Actually, I'm on light duty, but I had time off coming."

Her face turned pale, and he noted the trembling of her voice. No doubt the events had taken its toll. "Okay. I'd appreciate a ride."

She followed him, and he let her go by so he could shut the front door. A dog barked in the distance. Solomon. He'd forgotten about the dog. He'd probably be all right until the morning, but Silas would go get him after he got back from dropping Kennedy off. With the break-in and Liz being hurt, it'd be hard on the dog. Liz was seldom away.

"Is that Solomon?" Kennedy glanced at him after she buckled her seat belt.

"Yeah. I put him in his pen, but I'll get him after I drop you off at your house."

"Don't leave him locked up, please."

"You're right. I'm uncertain how long I will be gone. I'll let him out for now. He likes to patrol the area."

"What kind of dog is he? He's the biggest dog I've ever seen."

Silas smiled. Most people had that reaction. "A cross between great Dane and a mastiff. When Liz's husband became ill, and they realized he wouldn't live long, she and Wade discussed her living arrangements. She wanted to continue to stay in the country in their home but was nervous and wanted protection. Two days later, Wade came home with Solomon, a nine-month-old *pup*—" he made air quotes with his fingers "—he'd found at the shelter. Evidently the dog was too big and clumsy for the previous owner's younger three children."

"Aw. That's sad. But I'm glad Wade adopted him."

"Yeah. Wade took him to the local pet store for training class and taught him basic commands. Thing is, Solomon was a natural and wanted to please. I remember Wade telling me that to reward the dog, instead of treats, he performed for just petting and loving."

"Yes, dogs are wonderful at loving you."

The wistfulness in her tone made him curious about the statement.

She turned to him. "I probably didn't sound appreciative earlier, but I truly am thankful that you heard my yell for help. I don't know what I would've done if you hadn't been home."

"No problem." He pulled into Liz's driveway and quickly let Solomon out of his pen. Liz let the animal roam outside before bringing him for the night. When Silas got back in the truck, Kennedy turned to him.

"Will the dog be all right?"

Silas was wondering the same thing. "He's

used to being out for short periods of time, so he should be all right until I get back."

She sighed.

He finally asked, "Would you rather I bring Solomon with us?"

Without hesitation, she said, "Yes. Bring the dog with us. The poor thing was already upset at the guy for being in the house and now with his owner being gone."

"You're right. Liz is almost never away overnight." He got out of his truck and whistled. "Here, boy. Come on, Solomon." The big dog ran to him with his tail wagging and leaped into the back seat. Silas shut the door and climbed back in.

Kennedy's eyes glistened as she stared at the massive face leaning over the seat with his tongue hanging out. "Is it okay if I pet him?"

"Are you kidding? Solomon eats up loving."

She held up her hand and let the big goof smell her hand before she rubbed the side of his neck. "Hello, Solomon. You're a pretty boy. Aren't you?"

The dog stretched closer, and his tail thumped against the back seat. No doubt, the colossal canine would like to climb over the seat and sit in her lap if allowed. Silas shook his head. "He doesn't scare you at all, does he?"

She laughed. "He may be gigantic, but he seems like a big softy."

Okay. Silas had never thought of the dog that way.

She continued to pet the dog's head. "He didn't look like a softy when he attacked the guy."

"I've never known Solomon to hurt anyone, but it makes sense. Liz is his everything."

"Good boy. Such a pretty thing." Kennedy continued to fawn over the canine.

Silas shook his head. "You're going to have him acting like a baby."

"He is a big baby. He enjoys it."

Silas turned left onto the main highway.

Besides occasionally offering kind mumblings to the dog, Kennedy was quiet, no doubt thinking over the events of tonight. He had said little, but he knew she had to be considering the possibility she was Harper.

"How was Mrs. Barclay?" Her voice cut through the silence of the cab.

"Hospital personnel were still doing evaluations when I was there. It wouldn't surprise me if it takes several hours or more to hear back with results. Her son and daughter will be here in a couple of days to be with her."

"She has two more kids?"

The implications were not missed. Kennedy had a younger brother and sister, but he kept his comment neutral. "Yes. Dax would be eighteen months younger than Harper. Shasta, about four years younger."

She seemed to consider this but didn't respond.

How much should he tell her? Were they better off getting everything out in the open, or should he wait until she asked? "A few months after Harper was taken, Liz became pregnant again with another girl, Shasta. I didn't realize it until I was older, but I'm sure the new baby was in response to losing her daughter. Anything to fill the gaping hole she had left in their lives."

Kennedy said nothing more, so he dropped the conversation. With her directions, he pulled into her drive. His headlights shone on a cabin-style, single-wide cedar mobile home with rosebushes and neat-as-a-pin landscaping. A single strand of blue Christmas lights lined the roof, and two poinsettias sat on the porch, one on each side of a yellow door. Through the front window, lights blinked on a Christmas tree. The quaint home fit her no-nonsense demeanor.

He didn't like leaving her alone, but since she only knew him from tonight, he doubted she wanted to have him stay to protect her. "I'd like to check out the house before I leave."

"Doesn't look like anyone's been here, but I'd feel better if you would."

He could sense her hesitancy and was glad she didn't ask him to leave without checking out the premises. "Good."

Solomon joined them as Silas followed her up the steps of the wooden deck and waited while she inserted her keys. The door swung open.

She looked at him with concern. "I always lock my door."

"Stay back." Removing his gun from the back of his jeans, he stepped into the house with the weapon raised. "Stay here."

"No way." She stayed on his heels, and Solomon on hers.

"Leave the lights off." He took his flashlight from its holder and shone it around. The Christmas tree flashed multicolors illuminating part of the room. If they turned on the house lights, it'd give an intruder a perfect view of them. Hopefully, the flashlight would momentarily blind anyone. He strode through the house, first across the living room and kitchen to the main bedroom. No sign of anyone. Then they headed back across the length of the home to the spare bedroom. Boxes were stacked in the corner, and an exercise bike that looked like it'd seen a lot of use filled the small space.

"Doesn't look like anyone's been here." Her voice shook. "I know I locked the door."

"I'm sure you did. You can turn on the lights now."

She flipped the switch. "Wasn't that other Texas Ranger here? Randolph. Do you think he came inside?"

He hated to crush her hopes, but Silas shook his head. "Randolph would never go into a person's home for something like this. But I could ask if it'd make you feel better."

She considered it. "I'd like to know."

It was well past midnight, so Silas sent a brief text to Randolph. He didn't know if his friend would still be up, but he received a reply almost immediately. Silas looked up. "He never got out of his truck."

Kennedy looked perturbed at the announcement, and Silas would do anything to take away her pain and worry. But more importantly, he must keep her safe. They needed to find out for certain if she was Harper. For years, he thought about solving the case of his kidnapped neighbor, but it had been a dream. Reality stood in front of him, and the fear and questions were not to be taken lightly. This was Kennedy's life. And no matter what he'd hoped, he'd never want to destroy someone's childhood memories unless it also was a dream come true for a grieving mother.

The situation needed to be handled delicately. "I can stay if you'd like."

"No." She didn't even pause before the reply.

"Do you have any way to protect yourself?"

She shifted uncomfortably. "Yes, I have a shotgun in my closet my dad gave me when I moved out on my own a couple of years ago."

"Do you have anything smaller that would be easier to handle?"

She sighed. "The gun was in case I needed to shoot a poisonous snake or scare someone away from a break-in during the middle of the night. Not ward off an assailant who had his sights on me."

"I get what you're saying."

"My daddy lives a mile up the road."

It sounded like there was a "but" to come; however, she didn't continue.

"I can leave Solomon with you."

At the mention of his name, the dog looked up at him and wagged his tail.

Kennedy stared at Solomon for a moment, evidently considering the offer. "I can't say I'm not tempted, but he's already been through enough tonight. He doesn't know me or my house."

"He seems to have already be taken with you."

"Don't say that." She rubbed her hand against Solomon's fur, causing the dog to lean against her leg. "I'd rather not."

Surprise struck him, for he thought she'd instantly bonded with the massive canine. But how well did he really know her?

One thing was for certain, he had many memories invested in this case. Too many hours of reviewing the files. Even though Liz rarely mentioned the tragedy anymore, he figured she must still wonder what happened to her daughter. Didn't friends and family tire of hearing about things such as this after a year or so? Everyone else's lives went on with a future. Liz must've bottled her feelings inside, making her feel alone, trying to live through the lives of her other two children.

Or had Liz moved on, and it was Silas who couldn't put the abduction behind him?

He needed to quit stalling. "You have my number if you need me."

"Wait. Your card was in my car. Can I have another one?"

He reached into his pocket and gave her a replacement. "Please, call no matter how insignificant it may seem."

"I will."

She walked him to the entry and waited for his truck to back out of the drive before closing the door. Silas kept his gaze on the home in his rearview mirror as much as Solomon's head would allow. Once he'd gone a half of a mile or so, he turned around and came back toward her home. He pulled into the drive of a pasture and turned around. He backed up enough where his truck should be partially blocked from the road and cut the lights.

He had no intention of leaving Kennedy unprotected with a gunman still on the loose.

FIVE

Kennedy checked the windows and doors one last time before heading to bed. Everything appeared normal. Whatever normal was. If she did turn out to be the girl from the cold case, her life would change drastically. She hoped it was a fluke that she looked like the age-progression photo of Harper. As she pulled back the covers and slid into bed, her mom's image emerged in her mind.

Her chest squeezed in pain, and her stomach tied in knots. She felt...*betrayed*. A little over a year ago, her mom passed away after a long battle with cancer. Kennedy had taken care of her—a feat that took its toll both mentally and physically. But she wouldn't have traded the time with her mom for the world.

Was it coincidence her mom volunteered at the Loving Heart Adoption Agency? Kennedy spent a couple of days per week during the summer months at the agency. She and the owner's daughter, Rosa, played in a back office that was stocked with toys. With Kennedy being homeschooled, she and Rosa had become good friends. Since Kennedy's parents were older when they had her, most of the couples they spent time with had older children, leaving Kennedy to hang out with the adults.

Solomon. A smile tugged at her lips. Kennedy would've loved to have kept the big, sweet dog with her tonight. The memory of Princess, a lovable Irish setter, invaded her mind. A local canine therapy group had loaned the dog to her family to ease her mom's stress and pain from the cancer. A week after her mom's passing, the group moved Princess to be with another cancer patient. The loss of Princess compounded the hole in Kennedy's heart from losing her mom. There was no warning. Someone had picked up Princess while Kennedy was back at her first day of work after the funeral.

She didn't even get to say goodbye.

Slivers of moonlight shone through the blinds and the alarm clock read one nineteen. Her fingers massaged her temples. Being sleep-deprived brought on delirium. Hopefully everything would look better in the morning.

Just because Kennedy looked like some computer-generated photo didn't mean her parents had been up to no good. The whole situation could be a sad, terrible coincidence. And Silas Boone had made it worse by believing Mrs. Barclay's intruder attacked because Kennedy was Harper from some twenty-six-year-old cold case.

It was time to get some sleep.

No—it was time to pray. She closed her eyes and took a deep breath. *Please, Lord, help keep me safe. Be with the doctors that tend to Elizabeth Barclay.* Her heart didn't want to say anything more, but she couldn't stop the thoughts from churning. *And please, help us learn what happened to Harper Barclay, no matter what the results are. Amen.*

For the next few hours, Kennedy tossed and turned in fitful sleep. She awoke a little after six in the morning as the sun peeked over the horizon. When she glanced out the window, nothing looked unusual. No gunmen. Not a Texas Ranger in sight.

A smile tugged at her lips.

Did Silas get her car out of the ditch last night? She needed to get it home. Bob, an older man from church, liked to piddle on automobiles, and surely, he wouldn't mind looking to see if anything was damaged.

She wanted to call the hospital to check on Mrs. Barclay's condition, but she doubted they'd divulge any information to a nonrelative. Well, Kennedy assumed she wasn't kin.

After a quick shower and throwing her clothes on, she'd just grabbed an energy bar for breakfast when something reflected across her kitchen wall. A glance out the window showed Silas's truck sitting in the drive.

Didn't this man sleep? Again, he wore jeans and a cowboy hat. She'd seen less appealing things in the early-morning hours. She swung the door open as he climbed the steps to her deck. "Do you have Solomon with you?"

"Good morning," Silas greeted her. "I left him with Keith Studerville, a neighboring rancher who Solomon knows well. The dog's size can be intimidating, and I didn't want to have to leave him in the cab if we needed to visit people."

"I hate that, but I understand." She held the door open. "Did you not sleep last night?"

The cowboy smiled back at her. "Not much. I parked your car at my house. Runs fine but the front passenger tire is flat, and a guy from the tire shop should have it changed after lunch sometime. The paint's scratched on the front fender. You must've run over something."

"Yeah," she replied. "Like trees and no telling what else in the ditch. But I will say, you're efficient. Thank you."

Silas was an instant friend, and that made her nervous. Her whole life she'd depended on her mom and dad almost exclusively. Kennedy had been homeschooled through her elementary school years, and her family had attended a small congregation to worship. Her extended family was almost nonexistent. As much as her parents loved and protected her, Kennedy had always fought that tied-down, I-can't-breathe feeling.

Even as a child, she remembered being fussed at by her parents for being too independent. Her mom told her she'd get in trouble someday if she didn't quit being so spontaneous.

Right out of high school, she'd taken a job at a local fast-food joint and moved into the dorm at the local community college while saving for a deposit on an apartment. Within six months of moving out, the doctors diagnosed her mom with cancer. Filled with shame, Kennedy moved back in to help with the housework and doctor visits. Even though she knew the cancer was not her fault, disgrace weighed on her for wanting to get out from underneath her parents' rule.

Even before her mom passed away, her dad began struggling with memory loss and uncharacteristic fits of anger. Kennedy had chalked it up to fatigue and the emotional toll of dealing with an ill spouse.

Within a year, Kennedy realized life was unpredictable and anyone could be taken away without notice. It was important not to lean heavily on others.

As helpful as Silas had been, she supposed most people would feel obliged to invite him into the house, but she wanted to be alone—have time to absorb all that had happened. When she counseled with clients, she tried to get them to step back, see the bigger picture and not become overwhelmed by what appeared in front of them.

But could Kennedy do as she asked of others? After he saved her, she couldn't very well turn Silas away. "Come on in."

He followed her to the kitchen counter, where he stood instead of taking a seat on a bar stool. "I have news from the hospital. Liz Barclay has minor bleeding on the brain, and they have put her in a medically induced coma. Prognosis is good, but the doctors won't know anything for certain until the swelling goes down. Also, I called my lieutenant last night, and officially the Texas Rangers are working Harper's cold case."

"That's good news." That still didn't mean she believed she was the abducted girl. If

Harper were alive and out there somewhere, she needed to be found. "Is there anything else you need from me? You could've simply called."

He looked at her, his brown eye searching her face. With the patch over one eye, it made her want to lift it to see what he'd looked like without the obstruction. Shame on her for having such thoughts. But as the patch hid part of his features, she had the feeling the man also had secrets.

"First thing we need to know is if you're Harper. If you're not, then we'll know to move on. But…"

She held up her hand. "I get it." She scratched the back of her neck, irritation crawling all over her like a band of ants. "What would you like for me to do?"

"You can take a DNA test, but we'd have to match it against something."

So cold and technical. "I can take one, and I should be able to get something of my dads to compare it with."

"Since it can take weeks to get results, the circumstances may force us to move quicker instead of waiting. You mentioned your mom had passed away. Can you ask your dad if you were adopted?"

They were moving too fast. She hadn't mentioned her dad's forgetfulness to anyone. Did she really want to upset him right now? Defensiveness crawled over her. "I'd rather not."

Silas looked thoughtful for a minute. "Is there anyone else in your family who would know if you were adopted? An aunt or a grandma?"

She shook her head. "My parents were older when they had me, and my grandparents died before I was born." As the words poured from her lips, she realized it sounded like her parents couldn't have kids, so they kidnapped one. No way. The thought was ludicrous. "I have one aunt from mom's side that lives in Alabama and two uncles from dad's side that have both passed on. I've only met my aunt a couple of times, but I can try to find her number and call her."

Silas didn't look satisfied but nodded. "That's a start."

When she glanced down, the long scratch on her arm seemed to mock her. Elizabeth Barclay fought for her life in a hospital bed, and the same man who had attacked Liz ran Kennedy's car off the road, shot at her, and forced her and Silas off the bridge over the Red River. As much as she wanted to pretend none of this had happened, she had to take it seriously and face it straight on. "I'll talk to my dad."

Silas didn't go on, for which she was thankful.

"My dad lives just a mile up the road."

"I'm assuming you'd prefer to talk to him in person?" At her nod, he added, "I'll be in the truck."

She grabbed her purse from the counter, locked the house up tight and headed out the door. If there were any other way to avoid this, she would.

Traitor.

That's how Kennedy felt as they pulled into her dad's driveway. Her father had just lost his wife of forty-two years and here she was, their only daughter, not only suspecting him of deceiving her, but possibly committing an unspeakable crime.

Her gaze lit on the boat parked in front of the shed, and she suddenly remembered he was supposed to go fishing this morning. Why was her dad still here? Had something happened?

Surely the gunman hadn't come after her dad last night.

Silas noticed the blood drain from Kennedy's face as soon as they pulled in. "What's wrong?"

"My dad." She flung the door open, jogged to the porch and disappeared through the front door.

Silas surveyed their surroundings as he approached the modest home. A boat sat in the drive and a newer model pickup was parked under the carport. A large mimosa stood beside the house, and neglected flower beds ran along the front. Nothing appeared amiss, but he didn't know the man. Mumblings reached his ears as he stood at the door. "Kennedy?"

"Come on in," she hollered.

Silas stepped in and a musty smell assaulted him. Kennedy and a gray-haired man seemed to be in an intense conversation in the kitchen. Silas kept his distance in the living room to give them some privacy and took a seat on the couch. Overall, the place was cluttered, the curtains drawn, and dishes sat on the coffee table. Kennedy had mentioned her mom passing away, and Silas wondered if her dad were struggling. Depression wasn't uncommon when a someone lost a spouse.

"I wasn't supposed to go fishing until tomorrow." The older man's voice carried to Silas.

"Dad, the date was today. It's Thursday." Frustration laced Kennedy's voice. She glanced at the floor and stared for a moment, like she tried to collect herself. "I'm sorry, Dad. I had a rough night."

He frowned. "Stay up too late watching television? I've tried to tell you if you stay up looking at junk before going to bed, it'll keep you awake. Then you won't be worth anything come morning."

"My awful night has nothing to do with TV. I was supposed to visit someone about a kidnapping from twenty-six years ago. A cold case. I found an injured woman and an intruder in her house when I got there."

The man ambled into the living room, leaving Kennedy to follow. "I still say if you'd go to bed earlier, you'd rest better."

"You're not listening, Dad. I told you, I wasn't watching anything."

The man stiffened, and his jaw jutted. "Nonsense."

This wouldn't be a good time for Kennedy to question him about the kidnapping or adoption. He could see the respect she had for her dad, and it impressed him. Silas hadn't spoken with his own dad for over eight years, and he didn't know if they could ever mend fences. The last time they'd talked had been a yelling match over Silas joining the Texas Rangers and ended with his dad telling Silas to get out of his home and don't ever come back. Silas hoped Kennedy wouldn't mind, but he stood and interjected, "Sir, is there anything I can do for you?"

Her dad looked at him like he'd just noticed him in the room. "What are you asking?"

Silas held his hand out. "Silas Boone. I'm a friend of Kennedy's."

"Verne Wells." Wrinkles and calluses covered the older man's hands, showing a lifetime of work.

"Do you need any help with anything in the house? I couldn't help but notice you had a large branch rubbing against your roof."

"Why, sure." A smile spread across Verne's face in approval.

Silas glanced at Kennedy, and he could see the questions in her eyes.

"When the wind is up, that branch keeps me up at night. I've got a chain saw in the garage, but I can't get the thing started. Probably needs a tune-up. I don't mind cutting the limb if you'd get the saw going for me."

"I can do that." Silas followed him to the back door but paused when he got to Kennedy. He whispered, "I thought it might help if he calmed down before you questioned him."

"Good idea." She nodded. "I got scared when I saw his boat in the drive and thought something might have happened to him. You know, like our guy from last night paid Dad a visit. I wasn't thinking."

"You're the concerned daughter. That's perfectly natural."

Kennedy's dad was digging through tools and gadgets when Silas stepped in the garage.

"Here it is. Now if you could just get it started." Verne pointed. "You see that branch out there? That's the one."

"I do. Let me see what you have here." Silas filled the chain saw with gas and oil and brought it outside. On the third pull, the engine revved to life. "Can you get me that ladder?"

"Sure." The man hurried to lean the ladder against the side of the house.

Silas climbed it before the man had time to ask for the saw. He cut the limb, and the branch fell to the ground with a rumble. While he was up there, he trimmed another couple of branches that would soon be a nuisance.

"I appreciate this, young man."

"You're welcome, sir." Even in the cool weather, sweat trickled down Silas's forehead, and he wiped it on his sleeve. Then he returned the chain saw to the garage and pulled the cap off the spark plug. He didn't like being sneaky, but he also didn't want the man to get hurt if he tried to use it later. He turned to Kennedy. "I could use a glass of ice water if it's not too much trouble."

"Of course." She locked gazes with him before she asked her dad if he'd like a drink. When he agreed, she went inside.

Silas let out a low whistle. "Nice boat."

"Yeah?" He gave Silas a second glance. "You fish?"

"Sometimes. My grandfather used to take me when I was a kid." His dad never liked to fish, but his grandfather allowed him to fish in a stock tank on their place as often as he wanted.

Her dad chuckled. "I tried taking Kennedy when she was a little girl, but she didn't care for it. Using live worms disgusted her, so I bought plastic ones. You and I both know the fake ones don't work as well. Then one day when she sat still long enough to catch a fish and reel it in, she screamed and dropped the pole. She never wanted to fish again."

Both of them laughed as Kennedy returned with two glasses of ice water.

Verne grabbed a five-gallon bucket from the garage and turned it upside to use as a chair. Silas did the same with another container.

She handed each of them a drink. "What did I miss?"

Silas smiled. "Your dad told me about the time he took you fishing when you were little."

"I've heard that story a hundred times." She shook her head and smiled. "How old was I, Dad?"

He studied her. "You couldn't have been

older than two." He held his hand held at knee-level. "About that high."

A smile crossed her face.

Harper was abducted at three. Was Silas wrong about Kennedy being the girl?

Verne climbed to his feet, handed her the empty glass and stepped inside the garage. "I have things to do. I need to trim the limbs off the mimosa tree. The branches scrape the roof at night and keeps me awake."

Kennedy touched his arm. "Dad, Silas just cut those branches for you."

Her dad's face scrunched up into a frown. "He did?"

"Yeah, remember?" She pointed to the limbs on the ground.

He blinked several times, and then realization hit. An awkward smile crossed his lips. "Of course. I was just teasing. I have so many things that need to be done that I lose track."

After her dad went deeper into the garage and out of hearing range, she turned to Silas. "I know what you've got to be thinking, but the story he told about the fish is true. I've heard it my whole life."

Silas put his hands in the air. "I'm not accusing your dad of anything. He's a nice man."

"Yes, he is." She frowned. "I'll try to talk to him now."

Silas put his bucket away but looked away as she approached her father. This was an impossible situation.

"Daddy?"

He didn't look up. "What?"

"I need to ask you something important."

He could only imagine how difficult it was to have this conversation. Temptation to offer his support by moving beside her tugged at him, but he resisted.

"What is it, hon?"

"Did you and Mom… Uh. Was I adopted?"

"What?" Red flashed across his face. "Who told you that lie? Who have you been talking to?"

The vehemence in the elder man's voice didn't surprise Silas. But the way Kennedy flinched and the hurt in her eyes said her dad's reaction must've come as a shock.

"No one… It's just that while working a case, I went to see a lady last night by the name of Elizabeth Barclay." Kennedy talked fast, like if she didn't, she might not get the words out. "Someone kidnapped her little girl twenty-something years ago. But when I got there—"

"Enough!" He screamed and tossed his hands in the air. "I won't listen to you mar your mother's memories. I'm ashamed you even asked such a question. You're my and your mother's child. Adopted." He spat the word as if it was filthy. "Pff. You make me so mad I could spit."

Silas moved in front of Kennedy. It might not be his place, but he could see the damage her father's reaction was doing to her. "Sir, we'll be going now. It was good to meet you."

"What? Oh. Yes, same to you." The change in subject clearly threw him off. "Come by anytime." He wagged his finger at her. "And you're welcome to come, too."

"Goodbye, Daddy. I'll talk to you later." Kennedy swallowed as if she struggled to get the words out.

"Goodbye, baby. Glad you dropped by."

Awkwardness hung in the morning air as Silas and Kennedy hurried to his truck. Once they had backed out of the driveway, he broke the silence. "I'm sorry about that."

"My dad's not doing well."

Silas reached across the console and squeezed her hand. "I know."

"I didn't expect him to get so angry. He's always been so even-tempered and sweet." Kennedy blinked back tears, but it didn't stop her lip from trembling. "I'm not marring my mother's memory."

He slowed to a stop in front of her house. "I didn't believe you were. I don't know your father, but it appears he's suffering from dementia. The forgetfulness. The anger." Silas said nothing more about her father. It was clear she was upset. Her father didn't like being questioned about Kennedy being adopted. Did the question insult him, or was he a man with something to hide?

"Daddy doesn't want to see a doctor, but I don't think we have a choice anymore. Maybe there's some medication that can help." Her hand went to the door handle. "I appreciate you helping my dad cut that tree. It was a good attempt to get his mind on something else. I wished it would've worked."

"Kennedy, I'd rather you not be alone just yet. Give me a day or two to learn your identity. If you're not Harper, then fine. Go your way." Even as he didn't like the idea of not seeing her again. But what reason could he give for wanting to be involved in her life if she wasn't Elizabeth's child? She worked for the Bring the Children Home Project, so they could still work the case together. Yes, he decided, they had until this case solved.

She shook her head. "Thanks, Silas. Truly. But I can't wait around with my life on hold. I'll be careful." Before he could say anything more, she shut the door. He watched her stalk across the paved road to her house and disappear behind the door. After a few moments to make certain she wouldn't change her mind, he pulled down the road.

They shouldn't have questioned her dad when it was clear he wasn't doing well. Silas had only wanted to gauge his reaction to the question. He was 90 percent convinced Kennedy was Harper, but he needed to prove it to her.

She couldn't go anywhere without a car. He headed back to town to see how Liz was doing, and hopefully speak with her other two kids, Dax and Shasta. How would they take learning their lost sister had returned?

SIX

Kennedy watched Silas drive away from the window. Tears fell freely down her cheeks. Even though she knew her dad had been struggling with confusion, the stab in her heart at his rage still hurt. Daddy had never talked to her with such disdain. Had he already forgotten about her question, or would he grow even more agitated?

And being pursued by a gunman last night only added to the fuel.

Five minutes later, the tears had dried, and she put the scene in perspective. Her dad had been caught off guard by her question, on top of losing his wife and wrestling with health issues. Kennedy had thought she was prepared, but she hadn't thoroughly considered how her dad might feel.

You're my and your mother's child. Those were the words Kennedy yearned to hear, and she prayed they were true.

After making certain the front door was locked, she padded to her bathroom to finish getting dressed for the day. Anything to feel normal and not like her life was spinning out of control. Then she would see about getting Silas to deliver her car, but then she realized that he'd mentioned something about tires. She assumed until she replaced or repaired the tire, her car would remain undrivable. She could call a wrecker later this morning to deliver it to a tire shop.

What was wrong with her that she desired the Texas Ranger's help? Was it possible she was trying to involve Silas so she could see him again?

Ridiculous.

Even at the thought, she knew she'd leaned on him the past twelve hours. Twelve hours. What could she even know about the man? What she did know was that she couldn't depend on one person too much. That's what had caused her near meltdown after losing her mother. Besides God, she needed to be more independent and not rely on others.

Besides working at family-owned Stone River Counseling, she worked with some of the best people in law enforcement weekly with the Bring the Children Home Project. That's what was missing. She needed her team. She'd call them as soon as she dressed.

She plugged in her curling iron and dug out her makeup while it heated. Even though some of her team members had gone through dangerous or tumultuous situations, Kennedy had managed to stay at a safe distance from gunfire or waking up on a cliff with amnesia like Annie Tillman, the team's weapons instructor. In all those cases, the team had pulled together and came out all right on the other side. A team was better than putting all your marbles on one or two people.

After lightly applying mascara and a light-colored lipstick, she quickly began to curl the right side of her hair. Early-morning fog tended to cause her hair to frizz like today.

A glance to the mirror showed her mascara had smeared. She turned on the sink and dipped her finger in the stream.

A thump sounded somewhere in her house.

Her lungs froze.

Had she imagined it? Maybe. Leaving the water running to keep the noise audible, she peeked around the corner but saw and heard nothing.

Her heart throbbed in her chest.

Creak.

The noise came from outside her bedroom.

With her body shaking, she tiptoed into her room. The shotgun her daddy gave her sat in her closet. She'd placed the ammunition on the top shelf, so she didn't accidentally knock over the gun while trying to find a shoe or something and blow a hole in the side of her house.

A shadow moved across the door opening.

Not concerned with being quiet any longer, she slung open her closet door and grabbed the shotgun.

A masked man stepped into her bedroom. It was the same brown mask as the man wore last night in Barclay's house.

Her heart leaped into her throat, sending her adrenaline into overdrive. She screamed, "Get back!"

The gun was empty, but he couldn't know that.

Through the mouth opening of the mask, a smirk crossed his chapped lips as he wielded a pistol. Besides last night, she didn't think she'd seen the man before. He looked to be in his twenties, with dark oily hair sticking out from underneath the mask and a thin mustache that again brought attention to his apparent youth.

"Darlin', you have to cock the hammer before you can shoot."

Panic surged as he pointed his weapon, and she swung the shotgun like a baseball bat, striking him in the face. He crashed into the wall and his gun fell into the closet. Without waiting to see if she'd caused him damage, she dashed for the door.

His hand shot out and grabbed her leg.

She squealed and jerked, trying to free herself. His hand skidded down to her ankle, but she didn't stop jerking.

Finally, she was free and sprinting through the house. Pounding footsteps followed her. The glass door cracked as she crashed through it and leaped from the deck. She fell, her nose smacking the ground. Screams escaped her.

"You're gonna pay for that." Blood dripped from the man's jaw, giving him an even more evil appearance, his eyes wild with fury.

As he reared back his fist, she ducked and covered her face with her hands.

Tires squealed on pavement.

A glancing blow hit her shoulder, and she continued to curl into a ball. The man's weight pinned her down, making it impossible to escape.

"Get off of her!" Her dad's voice came from somewhere.

Suddenly the weight lifted from her torso, and a blur of movement had her trying to scramble to her feet.

She looked up in time to see her dad swing

his fist at the man's face, but the intruder dodged the attack and rammed his head like a football player into her dad's stomach, sending him falling backward to the ground with a thud.

The man sprinted across the yard and disappeared into the pasture behind her place.

"Dad!" Kennedy knelt beside him. "Are you okay?"

He clung to his stomach and gasped for air.

An engine revved and then quickly faded in the distance, but Kennedy's attention was on her father, who was writhing in pain. She put her hand on his shoulder. "I'll be right back. I'm going to call for help."

"I'm fine."

No, he wasn't fine. Kennedy dashed up the porch and into the house. She grabbed her cell phone from the nightstand and immediately called Silas. "Can you help us?"

"Where are you?"

"My house. Someone broke into my house while I was getting dressed. I tried to escape, but he caught me in the yard. If my dad hadn't been driving by…" She tried to swallow down the emotion, but her throat wouldn't comply. Her voice came out hoarse. "Daddy is hurt."

"Already on my way. Will be there in a minute. Stay with your dad. I'll call paramedics."

She disconnected and hurried outside. "Silas is on the way."

"I'm fine." He waved his hand, but even with the claim, her daddy closed his eyes, and his breath came in ragged beats. What had she gotten herself into? Why was this guy targeting her?

Even as she asked, she knew the answer. Someone believed she was Harper Barclay. Her daddy had said she wasn't adopted. A deep pounding throbbed through her head.

She wanted to believe the man who'd just risked his life to save her. Guilt plagued her for doubting his word.

But the question that flashed in three enormous red letters was why? If she weren't that little girl, why was that man trying to hurt her? He hadn't asked for anything or warned her away from the cold case. Was it a case of mistaken identity?

Silas's truck whipped into the drive, and a second later he was at her side. "Paramedics are on their way. How are you feeling, Mr. Wells?"

"Fitter than a horse." He put his hand on the ground and tried to push up.

"No doubt you are." Silas only half smiled as he put his palm on her dad's shoulder. "Stay here. Please let the paramedics check you out. Just to ease my and Kennedy's minds."

Kennedy looked at the Ranger. It didn't escape her attention how the man was aware of her daddy's pride, and respect for the cowboy grew.

For the second time in the last twenty-four hours, Silas watched an ambulance pull up. He stood back to give them room. Kennedy had gone inside to get her dad a jacket to ward off the chill. He didn't think the older man was seriously hurt, but he'd feel better hearing that from a medical professional.

It was time to learn who was behind the attacks. What was this guy after?

While Verne was being checked out, he called the sheriff's department. The dispatcher immediately transferred him to Deputy Trumble. He shoved mild irritation to the back of his mind, for it was probably better this way since the Texas Rangers would be helping. He preferred dealing with a rookie than a defensive deputy who didn't want their input. Trumble took his report and promised he would look to see if anyone fit that description in their files.

It didn't take long for the two paramedics to check his vitals and condition. The younger ambulance attendant said, "Mr. Wells, we're going to transport you to the hospital for observation."

"Oh, no you're not. I've never spent a day in the hospital in my life, and I'm not about to start now." He shoved himself to a sitting position.

The older paramedic walked over to Silas and spoke quietly. "His blood pressure is elevated which is not surprising, considering the circumstances. We can't force him to go, but I think it'd do Mr. Wells good to get a doctor's opinion. He appears fine, but the hospital can run tests to know for certain."

Kennedy was back with the light jacket. Silas didn't know how long she'd been standing on the deck. She walked over. "What's going on?"

"I'm not going to the hospital to be treated like a pincushion," the older man snapped, and climbed to his feet. He lost his balance and leaned into the closet paramedic so he wouldn't go down. "It wasn't nothing but a punch to the stomach. If I'd had a board, that punk would've thought twice about swinging at me."

"Mr. Wells, we can't force you to come with us, but I wish you would."

"Daddy." Kennedy stepped up and held out the jacket. He swatted it away. "Please do as they ask."

He cocked his head at her, clearly not in the mood to be coddled. He addressed his daughter. "Who was that man and why was he here?"

Hesitantly, she stared. Silas could only imagine that she didn't want to open that can of worms again. Silas spoke up. "Mr. Wells, these paramedics only want what's best for you."

An aging man who is used to being strong and the leader of his home didn't react well to losing his health and having to lean on others—especially his daughter, whom he'd always taken care of. Silas's grandpa never suffered with dementia but had struggled when he could no longer drive or get about on the farm. It wasn't uncommon for him to take his frustrations out on those who tried to help him, like Silas. Kennedy's instinct would be to assist, but now might not be the time.

Her father threw his arms into the air. "I'm fine." He marched to his truck. "I'm going home."

Her dad turned his vehicle around without waiting for Kennedy to tell him goodbye. He kept his shoulders square, no doubt hoping to prove his competence. A few minutes later, the paramedics packed up and left.

Silas and Kennedy exchanged looks. Finally, Silas said, "He should be fine just driving to his house. I'll call Randolph to get him to monitor him. I was going to do that anyway since our attacker put your father in his sights."

Her face fell and her hand went to her forehead like she had a headache.

Silas asked, "Are you okay?"

"Yeah. But do you really think my dad may be in danger?"

"Possibly. Depends on who's behind the attacks and why. But I don't want to take the chance. It can't hurt to have someone looking out for him, anyway."

"Yeah. There's so much going on right now, I don't want to fret about my dad being a target because of me." Her face fell. "And I wish Ranger Randolph could help us find out who's behind the attacks. I'm sure he doesn't like watching an elderly person all day."

"He doesn't mind. Not all the Texas Rangers' duties are full of excitement."

A sad smile flashed. "You're right. I just feel like all this is my fault."

His hand went to her back. "None of this is your fault. How did this guy attack you? Were you outside?"

"No. He broke into my house while I was curling my hair. I grabbed the shotgun, but he knew it wasn't ready to fire, so I swung it like a baseball bat and hit him in the face. It knocked his gun into my closet floor."

"I'll need to turn in the gun for evidence. Maybe we can track down its owner." He smiled. "I'm sure you hitting the guy made him fighting mad."

"It did."

His eye met hers, and his hand slid to her lower back. A tingling shot through his fingers. He dropped his hand to his side. Maybe it's because he'd thought of Harper his entire life. As kids, he remembered Harper being a funny, sometimes pestering little girl. His world changed the day she was taken. The Barclays fell into a quiet existence. They still had Dax and soon had another baby after the abduction. Liz never babysat Silas anymore after that day.

He used to fantasize about saving the day by finding Harper and bringing her back so that life would go back to normal. From the bus window, he'd watched along the ditches and pastures for any sight of her. When he rode along streets, he used to wonder if she was locked in one of the houses. Even as a teenager, he'd pass by the park just for a look. It wasn't until he got older that he wondered if she were still alive.

With him being six years older, he'd taken on the role of watching after Harper, making certain she didn't get hurt. Liz may've been his babysitter, but Silas had tried to help as much as possible. Silas's dad was a petroleum engineer with an oil company, and when his mom went to work in the business office of a dental group, Liz had offered to sit for him. His grandparents watched him a day or two a week, but his granddad had a lot of work to do on the ranch and some of it was not safe, to have an active boy around heavy machinery.

Again, he prayed it wasn't wishful thinking on his part that Kennedy was Harper. Silas had always had his feet firmly planted on the ground as an adult and a Texas Ranger. He took every case personally, because to the victim's family it was, but never like this before.

"Would you like to come in? I'm at a loss." She reached up and felt of her head. "And my hair is only half curled. I'm sure I'm a sight."

Her hair hung to her shoulders and one side had a touch of curl while the other waved. With her button nose and little makeup, he found her appealing, but he knew how women preferred to appear put-together. He smiled. "You look fine."

She rolled her eyes.

"We need to call my lieutenant, so I'll do that if you want to finish getting dressed."

"Guess I should at least put on some shoes." She wriggled her toes.

Silas got the feeling she was trying to pull herself together and not appear rattled. After he collected the assailant's gun, he put it in a bag and in a locked box in his truck. Then he went back outside and called his superior.

"Lieutenant Adcock."

"This is Silas. I wanted to give you an update." Silas recounted the morning events.

His boss listened quietly. Being a patient man, Silas expected no less. "Ranger Randolph called last night to fill me in, but Boone, you know you're on light duty."

"Yes, sir. My injury shouldn't keep me from investigating this cold case." Since the case had gotten dangerous, it was possible Adcock would want him to do the legwork but not to get involved with the danger. He could be a liability risk if he were injured. "There's no one in the department who knows this case as well as I do."

"I realize the personal implications. You believe this is the same girl you witnessed abducted twentysomething years ago."

"Yes, sir." A long silence answered him, but Silas waited patiently, knowing he shouldn't press his boss.

"Keep me updated. I don't have to tell you not to compromise this case. You're a good Ranger, but there's a reason we don't like our officers to work a case that they can't see clearly."

"I understand." Silas clicked off. The Texas Rangers did have other things he could help with. He needed to find a place for Verne to go that would be safe, but not upset him emotionally.

Kennedy came out the front door in a sweatshirt, jeans and hot pink running shoes. "I'm ready. Have you had anything to eat?"

He nodded. "I grabbed a PowerBar and a cup of coffee earlier, but I'm getting hungry."

"Me, too. I'm starving."

"Come on. Let's take a ride, and we'll get something to eat on the way."

She climbed in and buckled her seat belt. "Where to?"

"Something to eat first. Have you ever come across anything suspicious? Like, do you have a birth certificate?"

A hesitant smile crossed her lips. "Yes. And before you ask, I have a Social Security card and had no problems getting my driver's license when I turned sixteen."

He held his hand up. "Okay. You said someone sent a file to the Bring the Children Home Project. Was it addressed to you?"

"Yes." She glanced up as in thought. "It was lying on my desk Tuesday morning when I came in. But Bliss, my boss, or anyone could've put it there."

"Where is it?"

"The main file is still on my desk, but I took pictures of some documents to keep on my phone. I don't like to lug around all that paperwork until we get everything on the computer."

"Let's go see who left it for you, and we can look at the file while we're there."

She shrugged. "Okay. I don't know what you're hoping to find, but it won't hurt to check."

He waited while she locked the house, and then they climbed into the truck. Kennedy was probably right. The file would hold no clues, but he wanted to check it out, anyway. "If you are Harper, then the person behind your abduction would have reasons to keep you from learning the truth. And you accidentally being the one to work the case would be a little too coincidental for me."

Facing a long prison sentence would make it beneficial to eliminate anyone who wanted to learn the truth about Harper's kidnapping. Or use someone like Kennedy's dad to threaten her to quit investigating.

SEVEN

Kennedy's stomach was tied in knots as they drove across town. They stopped at Hallie Ann's for a burger meal to go, but now she wasn't certain the hand-cut fries had been a smart choice for her nerves. The more time she had to consider the events, she thought it too coincidental for Harper's file to wind up on her desk. And there being no return address made it even more strange. Had the person mailed it? Or come into the office?

She had no memory of strange people stopping by. The file was lying on top of a pile of papers she needed to file when she came in Tuesday morning. She'd assumed one of her coworkers had placed it there.

After Silas entered the address to the Bring the Children Home Project into his GPS, a male voice with an Australian accent came across the speaker. Kennedy found she like the voice much better than the female one she used on her app. Sort of made her want to laugh at the attractive image her mind conjured up. She could've easily instructed Silas on the way to get to her office, but there was something calming about riding in the quiet cab without having to talk. Right now, she welcomed anything that helped her relax. A few minutes later, he pulled in and parked on the side of the building. Two other cars were in the parking lot. Her boss's SUV and Josie Hunt's four-door sedan.

"You recognize the cars?"

Kennedy nodded. "Yeah. A couple more people may show up since it's after eleven and someone may've gone to pick up lunch."

Her boss looked up from her corner office when they walked into the lobby. Kennedy called, "We came to look at the Barclay file."

"Hold up." Her boss held up a finger. Bliss whisked into the room and joined them as they made their way to Kennedy's office. Josie didn't look up as they passed by her office but remained busy on her laptop. Bliss was an attractive woman in her early forties with a touch of gray in her hair and body that said she exercised regularly.

"Josie told me you had another attack this morning?" At Kennedy's nod, concern was etched across her wrinkled brow, but her gaze returned to Silas. "And you must be Texas Ranger Boone?"

"Yes, ma'am. I'm Elizabeth Barclay's neighbor and heard the commotion last night from the intruder."

"Bliss Walker." She shook his offered hand.

Kennedy noted that her boss scrutinized him, but she couldn't read her look. Bliss was good at schooling her features. According to what Kennedy had heard from other coworkers, Bliss had worked with US Marshals for years before her husband and son went missing. Her husband had been found dead a few days later, but her son was still missing. With her expertise with the marshals, she opened the Bring the Children Home Project to help other families find their loved ones.

Bliss asked, "What are you hoping to find?"

"Anything that will help us figure out who attacked Mrs. Barclay." She hadn't mentioned to her boss that Silas believed her to be Harper Barclay. What if they were wrong? Did Kennedy need to know the truth before telling her boss her thoughts?

Kennedy picked up the file and handed it to Silas.

"Is this all?" he asked. "Did it come in an envelope?"

"Uh, I think so." She wrinkled her face and eyed the trash can. "Hold on."

Silas asked Bliss, "Do you know who left the Barclay case file on Kennedy's desk?"

"It wasn't me, but we can ask around. Sometimes Josie delivers the mail. Is there a reason you're asking?"

He paused while Kennedy slid on a pair of rubber gloves and retrieved a large Manila envelope from the trash can.

"I found it."

Silas glanced over her shoulder. "No return address."

The handwritten address contained Kennedy's name in care of the Bring the Children Home Project. "It has my name."

Bliss said, "Okay. Explain."

Kennedy drew a deep breath. "Silas has reason to believe I'm Harper Barclay. Whoever sent the file must've believed the same thing."

Bliss's eyes narrowed, but she did a good job of not showing a reaction, although Kennedy was certain the declaration surprised her boss. She stared at the Ranger for a moment. "What leads you to believe this?"

Kennedy intervened. "Silas was there when Harper was kidnapped, and he keeps an age-progression picture of what Harper would look like now."

"It's true," Silas said. "Kennedy looks just like Harper, and since the cold case file was sent to her, and both her and Liz were attacked, it's too much of a coincidence not to be connected. I'm on light duty because of an eye injury, but Lieutenant Adcock gave his permission to work the cold case."

"Lieutenant Adcock. Hmm." Bliss's voice trailed off. "Go ahead. See if you find anything, but Kennedy, you'll need to keep me informed. A possible new case came in about two hours ago. Chandler and Josie are gathering information as we speak. Being that this is a live case, it'll take precedence over a cold case."

Kennedy said, "I understand. I'll keep working the Barclay case until I hear otherwise"

Bliss was silent a moment. "I know this is personal to you. The rest of the team will try to handle this case without you unless absolutely necessary."

"Thank you."

"I'll be in my office if you need me." Bliss walked out of the room, leaving them alone.

Silas held out is his hand. "Can I see the envelope?"

"Sure. Put on gloves first."

He smiled. "I realize the importance of not contaminating evidence." While he gave the package a look, she went through the files.

She'd gone over the documents the two days prior to going to Barclay's place and noticed nothing new.

He held the envelope up to the light.

"What are you doing?"

"Do you see that?" He pointed to above the address.

Faint indentions appeared. "Yeah, but I can't make it out."

Silas strained at the writing. "That looks like a *c* and a *t*."

"Hold on. I always do this if I can't read something." She retrieved her phone from her purse and snapped a picture, and then enlarged it.

He glanced over her shoulder. "That's much better."

Even though she knew there was nothing to his move, she couldn't help but notice the closeness they shared. "That looks like Vic… wait… Victoria."

"I think you're right," he said, and swiped the picture to the left a little. "Rollins. Victoria Rollins. Does the name sound familiar?"

"No, I don't think so." She dropped the phone to her side. "Do you think that's who sent the file?"

He shrugged. "Possibly. Or it could be the name someone jotted down to pay a bill or any number of different reasons."

"True." She nodded. "But it's a good place to start. Let me see if there is a person by that name." She powered up the laptop on her desk.

"I'm always amazed how enlarging a photo on your phone can make things come in clearer."

She smiled. "A couple of years ago, I went with my mom to visit cemeteries of our ancestors. This was after the doctors diagnosed her with cancer. Anyway, many of the headstones were illegible, so I took pics on my phone and enlarged them. Not only does zooming in help, but the phone makes it clearer. It was amazing how much better we could read the names and dates."

As her laptop came to life, she sat in the cushioned office chair and typed the name into the search engine. Many names popped up on the screen, so she added Liberty, Texas, to the name. Only one name this time, and Kennedy clicked on it. The lady lived in a nearby town of Spring Bluff, about forty-five miles away. "That's got to be her. Let's go check her out."

Silas snapped a picture of the screen with his cell phone. "I agree."

Once they settled back in his truck, he asked, "Have you recalled any more signs that would indicate you were adopted?"

The question irked her, even though the evidence pointed that way. She knew he was just doing his job; even so, to dismiss her parents so easily seemed wrong. If only Silas had known her mom and dad before her mom took ill and her dad struggled. He would never question it. "No."

He glanced back out the windshield. "I'm not trying to be a jerk."

"I realize that. If you had only known my mom, you would've understood why the question seems ludicrous. She was the best person I know. Mom was involved in all my school activities. Never lost her temper with me. And then she volunteered at the adoption agency."

"What?" His head whipped around. "She worked at an adoption agency. Which one?"

Kennedy frowned. "Loving Heart Adoption Agency. You really think she would kidnap me and then work at a place that adopts children to parents who would do anything to have a child? Why not just adopt me?"

He schooled his facial expressions back under control. "I don't know. But it wouldn't hurt to check it out."

She shook her head. "My mom took me with her two days a week, and I played in the game room with Rosa, the owner's daughter." Even as she said the words, she knew Silas only thought that made her mom look more guilty.

He didn't understand how caring her mom had been. She volunteered because of her love for children, not some sinister motive.

What Silas was talking about was pure cruelty, to steal a person's child.

Don't let your emotions blind you from the truth. Only a month earlier, Kennedy had said those very words to a dad whose teenage daughter had gone missing. Thankfully, the man's daughter had been found a week later with her boyfriend in another state. Not the perfect situation, but at least the dad had brought his daughter home.

Kennedy held herself straight in the seat, ready to get this visit over with. Maybe Victoria could shed some light on the situation. Maybe she was a witness to the kidnapping who never came forward.

Since she had a few minutes on the drive, she pulled out her cell phone and did a quick search of Victoria on social media. Her image quickly pulled up, and Kennedy clicked on the information. A slender middle-aged woman. Her profile pic showed what appeared to be her husband and three younger adult children at a July Fourth celebration. That would've been five months ago.

She scrolled through the woman's information, but privacy settings kept her from viewing friends and personal data. Kennedy had hoped if she saw the woman in a photo, she might have some kind of recollection, but Victoria didn't look familiar.

As they turned into a modest, low-priced neighborhood, the houses whizzed past the window. She couldn't help but notice the old pickup filled with junk in the side yard, like it had sat there for years. The yard at another house stood overgrown in weeds looked like it hadn't been mowed, as if no one lived there. Silas pulled into the drive at the best-looking house on the street—gray siding with dark blue shutters. Blowup Christmas decorations lay deflated in the yard, and a sign made of lights read Merry Christmas.

"Here we are." He turned to Kennedy. "You're right, I didn't know your mom. I'll withhold all judgement until we have evidence if you'll do the same."

She didn't have to worry about there being evidence against her mom, but she nodded in agreement, anyway. "If I am Harper, then there's an explanation. I'm hoping we'll know more after a visit with the lady who sent the file."

Silas took the lead up the sidewalk to the front door. When he rapped on the wood, the door swung inward. He glanced at Kennedy, who shrugged, and then he took a step inside. "Hello. Victoria? Victoria Rollins. Texas Ranger Silas Boone here."

"She wasn't expecting us, so give her a minute. I'd hate to just walk in."

He nodded but took a quick survey of the yard and neighbors. He knocked again and repeated, "Victoria Rollins. I'm Texas Ranger Silas Boone. I'd like to ask you some questions."

She followed as Silas took another step inside. Her gaze caught two legs and barefoot feet on the ceramic tile floor. She gasped. "Silas."

"I see." He removed his gun from his holster. "Stay here and don't touch a thing."

She wished she were miles from here. He continued to go through the house, identifying himself, and then he removed his cell phone from its holder and called 9-1-1. Even though he wasn't on speaker, the emergency operator's voice carried to her. She watched Silas kneel beside the woman and place his fingers on her wrist, followed by her neck. Then he mumbled the words *bullet hole*.

Kennedy turned her back to the scene and stared blankly at the Merry Christmas sign. Nausea churned in her stomach, and it took everything in her might to keep her breakfast down. What was going on?

Why would someone shoot this woman? Is this what Kennedy had to look forward to? Was she next?

Silas looked over the scene, careful not to contaminate anything. A pair of neon green flip-flops lay a few feet away from the woman, like she had taken off at a run. Medical bills lay scattered on the table. Family photos decorated the walls. If he were correct, the woman was married and had three kids, somewhere in their teen years to young adult.

While he was waiting for the coroner, he called Ranger Randolph and Officer Trumble at the sheriff's department. Technically, this would be under Spring Bluff's jurisdiction, but he'd leave the county and city authorities to sort it out.

As soon as the coroner arrived, Silas stepped out of the house and found Kennedy sitting on the tailgate of his truck, her arms wrapped tightly around her midsection. "Are you okay?"

She didn't look at him. "I don't understand. Why me? Why is this happening? It was a normal day at work, and I went to do an intake. That's it. Now everything is falling apart."

"Hey," he said, cupping her chin and lifting gently. Tears brimmed her eyes. "This is not your fault."

She laughed in a not-funny way. "Sure feels like it. Someone attacked two people that I've never even met—one dead and the other in the hospital."

"Liz Barclay will be fine. You'll see." He didn't like the thought of his longtime neighbor dying. She was going to pull through. And he hoped to reunite her with her missing daughter. He stared into Kennedy's brown eyes, and his heart faltered. He allowed his hand to drop.

"Can you guarantee my father won't be hurt next?" Her voice cracked.

He drew a deep breath. "Kennedy, the Texas Rangers are going to do everything in our power to keep you and your father safe. Ranger Randolph is watching your father's house as we speak. The best way to keep him and you safe is to find who is behind the attacks."

"I don't doubt your abilities. It's just we don't even know who is targeting us. You said I had a brother and a sister. What about them? Are they in danger? And who else that we don't even know the connection? I had never even heard the name Victoria Rollins until today."

"Then we find out who's behind the attacks now."

She rolled her eyes. "You make it sound so easy."

Silas's phone rang. He glanced down. "Hold

on. It's Randolph." He swiped up to answer. "This is Boone."

"Two things. Just wanted to let you know a silver Chevrolet truck has driven by three times. I jotted down the license plate number and sent it in to Chasity Spears in the Texas Rangers office. The driver kept his head down, so I didn't get a good description."

"Where's Kennedy's dad?"

As soon as the words were out of his mouth, fear reflected in Kennedy's perceptive eyes.

"He made several trips to the garage trying to get the chain saw started, and then he went back inside."

"Has he noticed you yet?"

"I don't think so," Randolph replied.

Silas gave the other Ranger the rundown of finding Victoria Rollins in her house deceased.

Randolph asked, "I assume Chasity is also running a background on her?"

"You know it." Another glance at Kennedy said she was hanging on to every word. "Any update about Elizabeth Barclay?"

"Yes. That was the other thing I wanted to tell you. I just received a call from Dryden, who reported Liz is out of her coma."

"That's excellent news." Silas relayed the news to Kennedy and explained Luke Dryden was a Texas Ranger on the case.

She clamped her eyes tight and whispered, "Thank God for answering my prayer."

Randolph said, "You want me to continue watching Mr. Wells or go to the hospital to interview Mrs. Barclay?"

"Stay there, please. I'd like to see Liz for myself. We can assume Liz was the first person attacked unless Rollins's autopsy tells us something different."

"I'll continue monitoring Mr. Wells. And I agree about Mrs. Barclay being the first victim. But let's not assume and keep digging."

"Agreed." Silas clicked off and turned to Kennedy. "Randolph is going to keep an eye on your dad while I see Liz. Do you want to go?"

"Yeah, I need to." She nodded. "Silas, I'm scared. I'm afraid for my dad and myself. What am I saying? I'm afraid for everyone who's connected with me. I don't know if it's such a good idea to stay in my house any longer. I'd like my dad to be with me, too. And who's going to protect Mrs. Barclay? Now that she's out of a coma, won't she pose a bigger threat?"

"There's an officer stationed outside Liz's hospital room." Silas stared at her for a moment. "I agree we need a better place for you to stay. Some place easier to protect. But I've been thinking about your dad, also."

She stared at him, dread dancing in her eyes. "Yeah?"

He held up a hand. "Hear me out, and then you can throw daggers. Is there someplace your dad can go? You mentioned fishing. Does he fish with anyone who can keep him away a few days, away from danger? Someone that wouldn't make him suspicious?"

Her defenses melted. "That's a good idea. He goes fishing with a retired guy he went to school with, Frank Henry. Frank often goes to Beaver's Bend in Oklahoma about three hours from here. I'll even pay for the cabin rental, so there'll be no reason they can't go. Not only do Frank and Dad get along, but Frank would also be patient with Dad's dementia problems since his own wife suffered with it for several years."

"Perfect." If Verne was somewhere safe, Silas could spend his time looking after Kennedy. He was certain the danger would not go away on its own.

But first, he needed to find out if Liz could identify the person who attacked her.

EIGHT

Anticipation built in Kennedy as she and Silas headed to the hospital. Was it possible Mrs. Barclay would identify who assaulted her, and then this could all be over today?

Even though it had been less than twenty-four hours since she'd arrived at the Barclay home, it felt more like a lifetime. So many things, her life and others', were hanging in the balance.

"With Mrs. Barclay waking, do you think she'll be safe until we get there?"

"We got it covered. Luke Dryden, another Texas Ranger, is waiting on the premises and waiting for us to arrive."

"And she's being protected?"

"Yes."

She nodded. It seemed to take forever to get across town. A mixture of excitement and dread filled her. What if Liz was her mom? Would Kennedy lose her dad? Would her brother and sister accept her as part of the family? She'd never had siblings before, even though she used to dream of being part of a larger family.

Images of her mom's and dad's faces raced through her mind. There was the time Kennedy had a high fever, and her mom sat up with her all night. The day she'd come home crying because she'd gotten a bad grade on her science project. She had been one of those kids who worked hard in school and was upset if she got anything less than an A. Her dad had simply said, "Booger, it's okay not to be perfect all the time."

Those simple words had really hit home. Her parents had always taught her the scripture, *And whatsoever ye do, do it heartily, as to the Lord...* Kennedy had always felt like any mistake no matter how small was inexcusable. Her dad "got" her. While many kids complained about their parents, Kennedy could never understand it. She actually liked her folks, even if they did seem overprotective. They wanted what was best for her.

It's okay not to be perfect. The words hit her hard. Maybe her dad had something in his past he had done wrong. Is that why he understood?

They pulled into the parking lot, and Silas put the truck into Park. "Are you all right?"

She nodded. "Just thinking."

He gave her a second glance before coming around and opening the door for her. They walked beside each other into the building, so close his confidence seemed to rub off on her.

As they waited for the elevator, he looked directly at her. "Whatever we learn, I'll be here for you. We'll figure this out."

Together. He didn't say the word, but its implication hung in the air. As much as Kennedy wasn't interested in a relationship, it felt good—reassuring—to have someone by her side when her world was spinning out of control. But that was the problem, wasn't it? She needed to stand on her own.

As they stepped off the elevator, she saw the police officer positioned outside the door seated in a plastic chair. He glanced up as they approached.

"Texas Ranger Boone," Silas introduced himself.

"I was told to expect you. Go on in."

Kennedy allowed Silas to lead the way while she hung back. Her stomach twisted into knots, making her feel nauseous.

A woman dressed in Christmas-themed penguin scrubs motioned for them to come over. "Remember, Mrs. Barclay is weak and doesn't need to be too excited. Dr. Ross said to keep the visit short."

"Yes, ma'am," Silas answered.

Kennedy's gaze locked onto the woman in the bed. An IV was attached to her arm, a narrow bandage covered her forehead and a blood pressure cuff along with who knew what else ran to the machine beside her bed. Gray and slightly curly hair spilled over the pillow. The night of the attack, Kennedy had only briefly seen the woman before the paramedics arrived. Mrs. Barclay—possibly her mother—was a little smaller and weaker-looking than the pictures Kennedy had studied and memorized.

As much as Kennedy tried, she couldn't get her feet to move closer. This visit could change her life forever, and everything she thought her childhood to be.

"You're looking under the weather." Silas smiled and took the woman's hand into his.

"Silas Boone." Her eyes slowly blinked, but her voice came out strong. "Be nice or I'll give your mama a call and tell her what you're up to."

"You know it." He cleared his throat, and his expression lost all teasing. "Liz, tell me what happened."

Kennedy stood off to the side. For now, she was content observing. Waiting.

Waiting for what? She didn't know. For her world to come unwound. Or to have her mother back after being stolen?

Mrs. Barclay glanced up at the ceiling tiles and touched her forehead with the back of her hand. "I don't know. The doctor said someone knocked me upside the head."

"Do you remember anything?"

"I was waiting for someone. I can't remember who, but it was important. A pickup pulled into the drive and then around to the side of the house, and I thought it was my visitor." Mrs. Barclay frowned. "But it wasn't. There was a knock on the back door, which I thought was strange."

Silas rubbed her hand. "Did you recognize him, Liz?"

Kennedy froze in place and held her breath.

The patient's brow furrowed. "No, I'd never seen him before. I got a glimpse of him only a second prior to him grabbing a brown ski mask from his truck and putting it on."

She must've moved, for Mrs. Barclay looked directly at her. "Who are you?"

Kennedy swallowed, trying to moisten her throat under the scrutiny. "Kennedy Wells. I was the one you were supposed to meet."

"Wells. That's right, from the place that helps families find missing children. I remember now. You were to interview me about my Harper."

Kennedy stepped forward to the opposite side of the bed from Silas. "I was running late. Maybe if I could've been there earlier." Her words hung in the air.

Silas glanced at Kennedy and offered an approving nod before turning to Mrs. Barclay. "Can you tell me what else you remember? Like if the man said anything."

"Let me think. My head is still fuzzy. I don't like this feeling at all."

Silas smiled. "I know you don't. I've never known a stronger woman."

"Flattery will get you very little, young man. Actually, that's not true…" She smiled, but then it faded as she rubbed the bandage. "My head is very tender. I put Solomon in his room when I heard the vehicle. Once I answered the door and saw the scraggly man, I realized my mistake. No one ever messes with me with Solomon around."

Kennedy could believe that. The dog had a sweet disposition but was huge. If the colossal canine wanted to cause damage, it'd be extensive.

"That is for certain." Silas patted Liz's hand. "This is important. Did the man say anything? Ask anything?"

The nurse walked in. "I'm afraid your five minutes are up."

Silas smiled—a powerful weapon if Kennedy had ever seen one. He said, "I appreciate your patience. Just a couple of more questions?"

The nurse thought for a split second before she nodded. "Five more minutes, and then you need to go. She needs her rest."

"Thank you." After she walked out of the room, he continued. "Did the man say anything?"

Surprise lit on the woman's face, and then her gaze went back to Kennedy. "Yes, he did. He asked about you."

Kennedy swallowed as she searched the woman's features. A pretty older woman. Smart if she had to guess. Competent. Against her will, Kennedy couldn't help but search for signs to see if she resembled her. With her pale complexion and the bandage on her head, it was difficult to tell.

"What did he ask?" Silas prodded.

"The man questioned why you were meeting with me." Her gaze still held Kennedy. "When I told him you were going to interview me about Harper's kidnapping, he blew up. Told me I knew who you were, and I should've left the past in the past. That's the last thing I remember."

Kennedy's chest tightened, making it difficult to breathe. Surely it was all a mistake. How could she be certain? The DNA test.

Mrs. Barclay's eyebrows drew in as she studied her. "Why would he say I knew you?"

Kennedy's knees almost gave way, but she put her hand on the wall to keep her balance. *Because I might be your missing daughter.* "Do I look familiar?"

As the older woman's brow continued to furrow, Kennedy's emotions wreaked havoc as she held her breath. She didn't want Liz to recognize her as little Harper. Did she?

Awkward silence filled the room. The humming of a machine was the only sound. Silas glanced from Kennedy back to Liz.

"I don't think you're familiar. Well, maybe your eyes." Liz asked, "Should I know you?"

Kennedy took a step forward. He thought she was going to reach out and touch Liz, but she simply smiled. "I suppose not. Someone left your daughter's cold case file addressed to me on my desk. I thought maybe you had sent it to Bring the Children Home Project and found my name online. Sometimes families will reach out in hopes we can find their missing child."

"I didn't send the file. When you called, I

was surprised. Every few years, the local television will air an update on my girl. I suppose because stranger abductions are rare, especially in the small town of Liberty. The station interviewed me on the twenty-fifth anniversary, but the segment got cut short because one of the girls from the high school basketball team received a scholarship to play ball at Baylor."

Silas could see the questions dancing in Kennedy's eyes. He sensed she wanted to ask her if she looked like her daughter, to tell Liz her assumptions.

Kennedy asked, "Has there been any new information?"

"No. Silas witnessed the lady in the red dress nab Harper and throw her into a black van. I had taken Dax, my son, to the restroom. We had just started potty training, and he couldn't be trusted to hold it. Harper was playing happily, and I left her with Silas. If I could do that day over, I would. I should've made Harper go with me. Back in those days, we all knew everyone in town like family. We felt safe."

Noise sounded outside the door, and Silas knew their time was up. He hurried to ask, "Liz, have any strangers contacted you?"

She frowned. "No. What is this all about? Do you think the assault had to do with my interview?"

"All right," the nurse said, and walked into the room. "Time's up. I've let you stay longer than I should have."

"Yes, I'm afraid the attack may've had to do with Harper's cold case." Silas squeezed Liz's hand. "I will check on you later. But I don't want you to worry. There's an officer posted outside your door."

Kennedy moved closer to the bed and smiled. "It was good to meet you, Mrs. Barclay. I'm certain we'll be talking again."

The nurse's eyebrows shot up, as if her patience were wearing thin.

Silas tipped his hat to her. "I appreciate you letting us visit with Liz. Don't let the woman give you any trouble."

"That's enough out of you," Liz teased.

A smile tugged at his lips as he and Kennedy moved out of the room. They stepped into the hall, and he gave the officer posted outside the door a nod—an unspoken acknowledgment the man had the room under protection.

Silas stepped into the elevator, and he pushed the button for ground level.

"I like her."

Kennedy's matter-of-fact statement didn't surprise him. He'd known she would. Everyone liked Liz. "Now that you visited with her, do you have any recollections?"

"I'm not certain. More of a feeling than a memory."

The elevator doors opened, and they moved through the lobby. "What kind of feeling?"

"Like, I think you may be right. I believe the attack had to do with the cold case." She stepped down from the curb and onto the pavement to cross the street.

A silver pickup sat across the parking lot. Silas's hand shot out. "Hold on."

"What?" She glanced around without being too obvious.

"Follow me." Instead of heading toward his pickup, Silas walked to the right toward the parking garage. "A man is sitting in a silver pickup on the other side of the street."

Kennedy moved farther behind the concrete column and out of the sight of the pickup.

Silas hit Randolph's number. When the other Ranger answered, he gave him the description of the pickup.

"That's the same one that drove by Mr. Wells's place."

"How far away are you?"

"Fifteen minutes."

"We need to question this guy, but I don't want to wait. I didn't notice him following me on the way here, but I don't like him being near Liz, even with the officer inside."

"I agree. What about Dryden?"

"He's inside. He's good about staying out of sight. Are you certain there was only one man in the truck? If it's possible there were two men, I don't want to leave Liz vulnerable inside."

"There was only one."

"Okay. Dryden and I will see what this guy is up to. I'll let you know what we learn." After he clicked off, he called Dryden and asked him for backup.

Kennedy drew a deep breath. "What do I need to do?"

"Stay out of sight and wait for me to tell you when it's okay to come over."

"All right." She drew a deep breath. "I hope we learn something valuable from this guy."

"Me, too." He kept his attention between the dude in the truck and watching for Dryden coming out of the hospital. Why was the guy still sitting there? Had he seen them walk out, or was his attention on Silas's truck, waiting for them to return?

Dryden stepped out of the building and headed his way in the parking garage without looking around the lot, but Silas knew the other Ranger was always aware of his surroundings.

Two ladies walked up the sidewalk toward

the lobby doors. An SUV pulled up to the parking garage and turned on its turn signal, waiting for another vehicle to pass.

A glance at the guy in the truck showed he hadn't made a move.

The SUV turned into the garage and drove past Silas and Kennedy. Just as Dryden was in the middle of the road, a red sports car up the street nabbed Silas's attention.

A person waited in the driver's seat, but the windows were tinted. Silas couldn't make out the identity of the driver.

The car pulled away from the curb and sped toward Dryden.

Silas shouted. "Watch out." He withdrew his pistol from his waistband and aimed.

Dryden dove out of the way just as the car almost hit him and then sped away.

Silas didn't take a shot for fear of endangering bystanders. He turned to the silver pickup. Without looking at her, he called out to Kennedy, "Stay there."

He ran across the parking lot.

The guy behind the wheel turned to him, and their gazes locked. The kid couldn't be more than twenty. In his peripheral vision, Silas could see Dryden weaving through the parked cars on his right. The man started his truck.

"Stop." Silas pointed his weapon. "Put your hands on the wheel."

Dryden continued to move to the far side of the truck on the passenger side.

The guy's eyes grew wide. He grabbed something from the seat beside him.

Silas ducked behind the protection of an older three-quarter-ton truck.

Dryden stepped up to the passenger's window with his gun aimed. "Drop the weapon."

The kid turned and fired. Glass sprayed the ground.

Silas moved in with his Glock raised. He yanked open the driver's-side door, grabbed the young man by the arm and jerked him out. The dude fell to the ground. "Texas Ranger Silas Boone. Drop the gun."

Instead, the kid raised the weapon, and Silas kicked the man's hand, sending his gun skittering underneath his truck.

Dryden moved around to the back of the truck and held his gun aimed.

Silas slid his Glock into his holster and grabbed his handcuffs. He jerked the kid to his feet. The guy fought for his life, kicking and swinging his fists. Silas dodged a blow, but the next kick caught him in the shin, making him cringe with pain.

"That's enough." Dryden moved in and helped subdue him.

A minute later, they had the kid cuffed. Animosity radiated in the man's eyes. "I wasn't doin' nothing."

Ranger Randolph pulled into the parking lot. Silas was glad to have him here. When he strode over, Silas asked, "Is this the truck you saw at Wells's place?"

The Ranger gave him a head bob. "Sure is. Was he here watching for Kennedy?"

"I was not."

Silas figured this could take a while, but fear danced in the kid's eyes. Hopefully he'd start singing and tell who put him up to watching Kennedy and Verne Wells. Or maybe he was here to harm Liz. Either way, it was the first break they'd had.

NINE

Relief filled Kennedy as she watched the taillights of Frank Henry's dually, pulling a small
fishing boat, disappear up the road. Her dad
had argued at first until he realized he'd be
fishing for the next several days and Kennedy
had even paid for the cabin rental. Silas had
visited with her dad while he loaded his tackle
box and grabbed his fishing poles.

Kennedy made certain he had his medicines
and clothes packed. She'd given Frank Silas's
and Randolph's cell phone numbers in case he
couldn't reach her. This was her daddy's first
overnight fishing trip since before Mom got
sick. She said a prayer that everything went
all right.

Silas seemed to sense she needed a couple of
minutes to herself, which she appreciated. She
turned and walked back to her dad's house, the
home she'd grown up in. Mom had died, and

Dad wasn't doing well. How much longer until she was alone? The thought didn't settle well.

A lump formed in Kennedy's throat as guilt weighed heavily on her mind. She couldn't help but wonder if asking questions about whether she was adopted or not had put undue pressure on her dad. He'd been struggling and didn't need her adding to the pressure. Two years of misery after the cancer diagnosis her mom had suffered, had surgery to remove the tumor, and then took chemotherapy. Six months later, she received a clean bill of health. Nine months after that, the cancer was back and had spread—a roller-coaster ride of hopes followed by devastating news.

"You want to go in and check things out?"

She glanced up at the Ranger. They had discussed that with her dad out of town, it would be a good time to go through his office to see if there was any evidence of who was behind the attacks. Also, she wanted to find something that contained DNA, like a comb. While in town, they had stopped by a lab and gave a sample to have Kennedy's DNA tested. Now all they needed was something of her dad's. "Might as well get it over with."

"I just heard back from Dryden. The kid at the hospital in the silver truck is twenty-year-old Lyle Baker. Have you heard of him?"

"No. The name isn't familiar."

"He was charged with possession of marijuana and several speeding tickets. Not much of a criminal record, but they're still trying to get him to talk. So far, he's admitted to no wrongdoing."

Kennedy hoped they learned more, but it was good they had a name.

Silas kept his distance, letting her lead the way. "Where would your dad keep things? Documents or names and addresses?"

"That's easy. His office. My mom kept the rest of the house spick-and-span, but the only places my dad claimed as his own were his office and the garage."

"Okay. Want me to check out the garage? Or let's work together?"

If he were to go through the garage, she'd rather be with him. How would he realize if he found something? "Let's stick together."

"Okay."

First, she retrieved the comb from her dad's bathroom and gave it to Silas. Then she padded to the back of the house to her dad's office. The room was an absolute mess with things scattered everywhere. Unopened mail lay stacked on the desk. Some lay on the floor like it had fallen off. Had her dad been looking for something?

She sifted through what was mostly bills. When all of this was over, she'd come back over and help him go through everything and throw away the advertisements and junk mail.

A quick glance in the closet only produced a bundle of odds and ends, old stuff. An ancient projector and screen. Who knew if the thing even worked? A guitar leaned in the corner with a broken string that her dad hadn't played in years. On the floor lay a pile of ball caps her dad had collected, and a football signed by a player Kennedy had never heard of.

She sank into her dad's leather office chair that she remembered as a child. It was a rule to never play in her dad's office, but sometimes she'd go into the room to look for something and then nose around. A smile tugged at her lips. Why did kids never listen?

Her mom would catch her and then usher her from the room. Kennedy never knew why it was a big deal. Probably just bills and checks and tax stuff. The things that weren't a kid's business.

There was that time a couple of years ago when Daddy had caught her in his office while she was searching for an old magazine for her mom. The issue had a recipe in it that Mom wanted to make for Sunday dinner. After searching the desk and the pile of magazines and with no success, she saw something sticking out on a shelf. Her dad walked in and then went wild, destroying the room, claiming she had no right snooping. The outrage was out of character for him. Was there more to his outburst? Was he hiding something?

Her mom must've heard the commotion, but never commented. Maybe even then Daddy had been struggling with health problems.

Two large photograph albums lay on the desk. She grabbed the first one and ran her fingers across the blue vinyl cover trimmed in gold. She flipped it open, and photographs of her mom and dad dating stared back. They had been in high school at the time, a small school in east Texas about a three-hour drive from Liberty.

One of Kennedy's favorite pictures was the black-and-white photo of her mom wearing her dad's letter jacket, smiling, sitting in an old car. Her parents had been just kids when they started "going together." Names and dates had been written below most of the images. She turned the page again to their wedding pictures. Mom had said they'd gotten married by the justice of the peace since she was just eighteen.

A lone tear traveled down her cheek. Kennedy had viewed the albums with her mother numerous times as she lay dying in a hospital bed set up in the living room.

She released a heartfelt sigh. It seemed like yesterday. What she wouldn't do to hear her mom's voice or laugh one more time.

Finally, she set that book aside and grabbed the other album—the one that contained pictures of Kennedy when she was a kid. There were no baby pictures of Kennedy. Her mom had told her the house they'd rented had suffered an electrical short and caught on fire. Many of the keepsakes and photos had been destroyed.

She glanced back to her parents' album. But *their* photos had survived. Why was that? As a child, Kennedy had never questioned the fire story, but accepted that was the reason there were no baby pictures until she was around three.

An arrow to the heart pierced her. Had Mom made up the fire story? Had she lied to keep Kennedy from learning the truth? Of course, she had. Who confessed to kidnapping?

"You all right?"

"You scared me half to death." Her hand flew to her chest at Silas's voice. "I forgot you were in the room. Yes. Just reminiscing."

He strode over, and his gaze went to the album. "Anything interesting?"

"No. I've looked at these family photos my entire life, especially right before my mom's death. Haven't looked at them since then." She got to her feet, ready to get out of there.

A hand clamped down on her shoulder. "I'm sorry, Kennedy." His gaze connected with hers. "I know this has been hard on you. Just know if I could turn back the clock on your pain I would."

"Thanks. But none of this is your fault. I'm to the point where I want—no I *need*—to know the truth surrounding Harper's abduction. Good or bad." Even though she attempted to be strong, her voice cracked. "I have no baby pictures."

"What?"

She explained about the supposed fire, but her parents' albums surviving.

"I'm sorry." He pulled her into her arms and squeezed gently. She laid her head on his shoulder and inhaled the warmth and strength of his touch. It'd been a long time since she could lean on someone. After her mom was diagnosed, she'd felt the weight on her shoulders to take care of not only her mom, but her dad. So much, she even took several months off from work to tend to her. She'd leaned on God, and said prayers often, but every once in a while, it would have been nice to have someone wrap their arms around her. Like now.

Silas pressed his lips to the top of her head. "Everything will be okay."

He couldn't know that, but the words comforted her just the same. Just to hear reassurance was nice. Finally, she pulled away. "I guess we should go through more of this stuff before we get out of here."

She returned the albums to the bookshelf and shoved her dad's chair back under the desk. A glance to the mess—the drawers open and askew, books on the desk and the floor. Even her mom's sewing kit lay open and the contents emptied. Her eyes glazed over as she tried to figure out where to begin. *Just get it done.* With new resolution, she got to work on the drawers in the desk while Silas went through the books on the shelf.

Twenty minutes later, she stood and stretched her aching back. "I don't think my parents ever threw anything away. There's bank statements and checks dating back thirty years. Did you find anything?"

He shook his head. "Nothing. Looks like your dad read Westerns while your mom preferred the classics. No mysterious key or message hidden in any of them. And a quick go through in the closet didn't produce anything either."

Disappointment weighed heavy on her that

they had learned nothing. Been a waste of time. "I guess we can go."

As she turned to leave, her gaze went to Mom's doll on top of a bookcase.

I've had this baby doll ever since I was a little girl. I've always wanted to have kids. I want you to have it. Her mom's words replayed through Kennedy's mind, but her dad had walked into the room, cutting their conversation short.

I've always wanted to have kids. Was that an admission of not being able to have one?

Suddenly, Kennedy climbed on top of the desk.

"Wait. Be careful." Silas hurried to stabilize her as she retrieved the doll from the top shelf. He took her hand and helped her back safely to the ground.

The doll. A symbol of what Mom wanted. Wanted Kennedy to have it.

A quick examination of the toy showed nothing unusual. A raggedy coat covered the cotton blue dress, and Kennedy carefully pulled it off. Three long threads braided together hung from the back.

Could it be?

She pulled the thread, and the back of the doll opened. A plastic baggie was rolled neatly inside. Her heart stampeded against her chest.

She removed the bag and looked inside. Several pieces of paper. Kennedy's breath held as she unrolled the contents.

The larger piece of paper was a document from the Loving Heart Adoption Agency. A quick scan revealed several documents signed by a lawyer and judge for the adoption of Kennedy Anne Wells to Verne and Nicolette Wells. Her throat went dry, making it impossible to swallow. A slight slip of paper fell to the desk. A receipt from Glen Winsett of the adoption agency dated two weeks after Harper's abduction.

Kennedy sank to the floor.

So, it was all true. Her parents adopted her, but never told her. It was like one gigantic continuous lie her whole life. And even though she had been close to her mom, Kennedy had never been told the truth. Even on her mom's deathbed. Why?

Was it because they had kidnapped her?

Silas could see the moment everything changed in Kennedy. The blank expression—disbelief followed by an empty pain.

"Kennedy." He said her name, but she didn't look at him, so he said it again. "Kennedy. Are you okay?"

Still sitting on the floor, she didn't glance

at him. "It's true. I was adopted. Daddy paid $30,000 for me to the Loving Heart Adoption Agency. So not only did my mom and dad know, but everyone who worked at the agency. You'd think *I* would be included on that need-to-know list. It's not that adoption is such a bad thing. After all, I've witnessed many families brought together for different reasons, but why not simply tell me the truth?"

"*Truth.* Such a simple little word, but so destructive when we don't have it."

He knelt beside her and took her hand in his. "I'm sorry you had to find out this way. I can only imagine what you must feel." He patted her hand. "But don't jump to conclusions of bad intentions until you know. Your parents must've had their reasons."

"Like maybe I was kidnapped?" she snapped. "And they were in on it from the very beginning? Did Daddy hire that thug to attack me last night and my *real* mom so he could avoid jail?"

His chest squeezed with pain, wanting to take away the betrayal. "Kennedy, he paid an adoption agency. If he was behind the abduction at the park, I don't think he would've paid money as well. I'll do whatever I can to help you find the truth and deal with this. But—"

She snorted. "I'm the psychologist that people go to when they need help in dealing with kidnapping issues." She rubbed her forehead like she had a sudden headache. "I'm a mess and can't even deal with my own issues. How am I supposed to help others? Who am I?"

Tires on gravel sounded on the rock road outside.

"Kennedy. We must go."

"What?" Confusion overtook her expression.

He took her by the hand and pulled her to her feet. "We've got to go. Someone is after you," he said, as if she'd forgotten. And maybe she had.

A glance out the window showed a small blue pickup pulling into the drive. Different from the one earlier. How many assailants where there? "Come on. Out the back door."

He raced down the hallway and out the sliding patio door with her hand in his just as the front door burst open. Silas slid his Glock out of his waistband, put himself between the gunman and Kennedy, and pushed her toward the side yard. "Go. Around the side of the house."

Her eyes were wide and suddenly clear from the previous distraction. She took off.

It was time to put a stop to this now. He just wished he'd told Kennedy to call Randolph.

The man's gaze connected with his and surprise lit in his expression. The male couldn't be over thirty, and the way he sloppily carried himself and burst in with no plan said he was no professional. Was he expecting to find Kennedy alone? Or her father? He aimed. "Stop. Texas Ranger Silas Boone. Drop your weapon."

The gunman's scraggly blond hair fell into his face, blocking his view. His eyes darted about the room like he was looking for an escape.

Silas stepped back through the door, most of his body protected by the side of the house, but his gun arm aimed through the opening. The man raised his pistol. Silas shouted, "Don't do it."

Fear crossed the guy's face, but he continued to proceed.

Silas fired his weapon, hitting the man in the shoulder and spinning him around. "Drop your weapon."

The man lurched forward, dropping his gun as he clutched his shoulder. "No! Don't shoot! I ain't killed nobody."

Silas watched as the color drained from his face.

The man grunted and headed back out the front door, stumbling onto the porch.

Kennedy!

Silas chased the man, but the young assailant was more intent on getting away than on searching for Kennedy. Silas raised his gun. He could've easily shot him, but he didn't know Kennedy's location.

The man clambered to get in the truck and then he took off, the truck weaving down the road.

"Kennedy?" Silas rounded the house but didn't see her at first. But then her head peeked from around a huge pecan tree.

"Is it okay to come out? Was there only one guy?"

"Yes." Relief flooded him as crossed the yard to her, and she fell into his embrace.

She pulled back and looked heavenwardly. "When is this ever going to stop?"

"When we find out who's behind the attacks."

"But I didn't know this man." Sadness shadowed her eyes.

"I don't think this is the guy calling the shots. Someone else is. We need to find out who. Hopefully, we'll learn more from Lyle Baker."

"Okay. I'm willing to do whatever it takes."

He hoped she understood what she was saying. And Silas didn't believe in sugarcoating the truth. "Just know that this could get much worse before it gets better."

"Aw. You're just trying to make me feel better." Sarcasm laced her reply.

A smile came unbidden to his lips. At least she had a sense of humor. He had the feeling she was going to need every tool available to deal with everything.

"What's the next step?"

"Let's make a visit to the adoption agency."

Her face fell. Quickly, the move was replaced with a curt nod. "I'm with you."

TEN

Kennedy stared out of the window as the scenery raced by. Christmas lights and decorations decked most homes. Some proclaimed to have a Merry Christmas, others displayed a nativity scene.

Suddenly, her gaze locked onto her reflection in the glass.

Her life was a lie.

Silas didn't say a word as she stared out of the window. Once again, she examined her reflection. Who did she look like? A mixture of Elizabeth and Wade Barclay? Two strangers? Not strangers, but her parents. Her rightful parents. If she'd never been kidnapped, what would she have become? Would she have chosen a different career? Have a different personality?

Even if she didn't have a degree in psychology, she knew it did little good to dwell on the what-ifs. How could she not? Why had her mom, Nicolette Wells, worked at the adoption agency? Kennedy had always believed her own desire to work with Bring the Children Home Project was due to her mom's influence. What if it was because there was a part of her, her memory, that remembered she had been abducted?

Was that possible?

When she'd pulled into Liz's Barclay's drive, she'd thought the place looked familiar. Then there were the tall cedars. Did she remember the Christmas tree farm? Is that why she always wanted to buy one instead of use their artificial tree? Did she have memories of home?

The receipt had erased all doubt that she was adopted. Why thirty grand? Lawyer's fees and court documents would take money. But that much?

How did she put her life back together? Someone wanted her dead. Who? It must be the person with the most to lose—the strongest motive—the person behind her abduction. Her dad? Glen Winsett? The man in the mask didn't resemble her dad or Glen, but that didn't mean someone hadn't been paid to do the dirty work. Or was it someone else entirely?

"We'll find who's behind these attacks."

She jerked toward the sound of Silas's voice. It was as if he had read her mind.

No matter the cost—the danger, or if the truth led her to something painful beyond imagination—she intended to keep digging. Her life would be meaningless if she continued the lie.

"Yes, I intend to learn the truth."

His eye connected with hers, scrutinizing her as if trying to read her mind. There was no need. Kennedy realized the risks and accepted them. No one knew better than her, her life was changed forever.

Bliss had wanted Kennedy to keep her updated. She called her boss and let her know about finding the receipt and their plans to visit the agency.

"That's a good idea," Bliss responded. "Keep me in the loop. We're working the live case. A nine-year-old boy disappeared while riding his bike home from a friend's house late yesterday in the tiny place of Sheppard's Town. Jarvis County Sheriff's Department called me an hour ago to confirm the details. Continue working the Barclay cold case with the Texas Rangers, and I'll let you know if you're needed."

"Thank you."

Silas glanced across the cab at her, and she relayed the part of the conversation he couldn't hear. "A boy went missing while riding his bike home from a friend's house in Sheppard's Town yesterday."

A frown furrowed his brow. "I'm sorry to hear that. It must be a tough job, but I'm glad there are people like you out there helping these families."

"You mean families like mine." She held up her hand. "I don't mean to complain. Bad things happen to people every day. I see it and counsel victims and do everything I can to help. But I've always been able to distance myself. Although I try to put myself in these families' position, I really couldn't. Could I?"

"You can't know what you don't know."

She looked at the cowboy, amazed by the simpleness of his comment. She appreciated his common sense.

"Profound, huh?"

She laughed. Couldn't help herself. "Actually, it is."

"What happened to your eye?" Here she'd been running around the country with a man who'd risked life and limb to protect her, and she knew nothing about him.

He smiled, a cute dimple lighting up the right side of his face. There it was again. That dangerous, bad-boy look that she'd never been attracted to. Well, not openly, anyway. Somehow, he combined the dangerous look with a charming grin.

"I'd like to say I jumped on a bomb to save a helpless damsel in distress or even a stray dog from a burning three-story building..."

"But..."

"I was working a case down on the south side of Dallas. Not a safe neighborhood. Anyway, there wasn't supposed to be danger, but you always keep on guard if you want to stay alive." He nodded. "We were investigating a murder of a local man with possible gang ties. We were at the crime scene and the building was supposed to be clear."

"It wasn't?"

"When I stepped into the alley, in broad daylight mind you, some local teens shot off fireworks at us and got me right there." He touched his eye patch.

Her mouth dropped open. "Are you serious? That's so needless."

"Yes, it is. The fifteen-year-old kid was arrested. Wound up it was his third offense, and he'll spend the rest of his childhood in juvie."

"Seems like there should be a better way to help kids. Some run away. Some are abducted. And then kids like him get in trouble with the law before they ever reach adulthood."

"All we can do is work together to try to

make it a better and safer place. Ever since I saw you kidnapped from the park, all I've ever wanted to do was help people."

"Witnessing Harper, me, being abducted really affected you, didn't it?"

"It was the most helpless feeling in the world. I saw what it did to the Barclays. I wasn't that close to my parents, even less to my dad, but Wade and Liz had always been a happy family and good to me. It's like it drained the life right out of them. Wade had always been a good match for Liz—strongheaded, hard worker, had a good sense of humor. But after the lady kidnapped Harper from the park, they became reserved, not going out as much. Even as a child, I noticed it."

Kennedy could only imagine what it must've done to her family. The buzzing of her phone had her glancing down. A text from an unknown number.

This is Rosa. I have important information you need. Meet me at the lake house on Possom Creek Trail.

A lump formed in her throat as she read the message aloud for Silas.

"You've mentioned her earlier. This is owner of the adoption agency's daughter?"

"Yes. Glen Winsett's. We were the same age and used to play together when my mom would volunteer. We remained friends until we got old enough not to go to the agency. Going to different schools made it difficult, but occasionally we saw each other at events."

"And the lake house?"

"It's the one her daddy owns. Every summer, he'd throw a picnic and get-together for employees and volunteers from the agency."

"Let me call Randolph for backup."

Her hand touched his arm. "Wait. Is that necessary? Would you rather meet with Rosa first and see what's going on?"

He squinted in scrutiny at her. Finally, he said, "Okay. But I'm going to call and let him know what's going on. Tell him to head that way."

She nodded. As Silas put in the call to his partner, she thought about the text. Had Rosa been receiving threats or been attacked, too? Or had she simply heard about the assaults on Kennedy?

After he was off the phone, she looked up the lake property on GPS, but couldn't find the exact location. At least he had the name of the road. She was certain she'd remember how to get there when they were close.

"How well do you know Rosa now?"

She shrugged. "I don't anymore. But she was always a nice girl, and we got along great." As they had grown older, they had drifted apart because they each had new friends. But that was typical of many friendships. "Rosa married some cute guy a few years ago, and they just had a baby—a boy, I think. I only met her husband at their wedding, but it's hard to visit at events like that. Seems like Rosa has done well for herself."

Silas merely nodded.

As the roads snaked through overgrown woods and became more secluded, memories of visiting the lake with her family returned. Her mom always made a fruit salad and some kind of pie. When a lot of other families brought cookies or cupcakes, her mom's pies always seemed to be a hit. Sadness sat on Kennedy heavily. When Kennedy was young, she never appreciated the little things. She just thought it was a normal part of life. But now that her mom was gone, it hit her hard. If only she could've had a few more years to get to know her mom as an adult-to-adult relationship instead of that of a child.

And she'd love to ask her mom about the adoption. "Why had she kept it from her?" type of thing.

"Right there." She pointed to a run-down

shed. "One summer, when I was about ten, I got to spend three days with Rosa and her family, and we made a clubhouse in that shack."

Silas glanced at her; a grin tugged at his lips, but also reservation. Like he wanted to offer a warning.

She continued. "I was the club president since I was older by seven months, and Rosa was the treasurer."

"Had a lot of money, did you?"

She laughed. "No, not really. There were some old square bales of hay that we stacked to make walls of our cool house. We agreed when we got older, we'd live together and make that our house while in college. Needless to say, none of that happened as we grew up and went our separate ways."

Kennedy directed Silas to the lake property. Weeds had overtaken the place. Grass sprang up in the driveway. Shingles were missing on the roof, and the cedar shutters and trim showed signs of rot. "Aw. The place has gone downhill. And that tree house—" she pointed to the backyard "—is crumbling. I don't see how we even safely played up there. It's not as high as what I remember, either."

"I think that's common when we visit places from our childhood."

"I suppose you're right." But still. As the

memories flooded her, she glanced around. "I don't see any vehicles. Do you?"

"No. Do you know what she drives?"

She shook her head.

Silas slowed as he pulled between the house and the boathouse, no doubt so he could see most of the place and for an easy getaway if needed. "Kennedy, we don't know that was Rosa who texted you."

"That thought crossed my mind, too, but someone would have to know me well to write that message. I'm going to let her know we're here." She picked up her cell, but Silas stopped her.

"Wait. If Rosa didn't text you, we don't know who tried to get you here. Since we know you were kidnapped and then adopted out, Glen Winsett would be at the top of the list of suspects."

Annoyance seeped into her. "I realize that, too. But if you knew him…" She stopped herself, even though it was tearing her up inside. "You're right. The text could be a setup. I need to stop defending people no matter how close they are to me. But the message could be from Rosa, and she has information that's important."

Silas frowned. "I'm not trying to insult your family and friends."

"I know. I really do. I'm normally the patient, coolheaded one." She sighed and rubbed her neck. *Please, Lord, help me look at these events with a rational mind.* "This case is really getting to me. What do you want to do? Sit in the truck, or check things out?"

"Let's stay in the truck to see if someone shows. I don't like this."

"Okay. But maybe we're early. There was no meeting time on the text." Even as she said the words, she realized she sounded in denial. Or at least that was what she'd think if she were listening to a client talk about their situation.

Silas glanced her way before turning his attention back to the premises. He checked his rearview mirror for the third time, she supposed to make certain no one came up behind them. "I'm going to let Randolph know what's going on."

She waited until he sent the text. "Do you think Rosa could be in danger? After seeing what happened to Victoria Rollins, I don't know what I would do if they found Rosa injured. Stay far away from everyone I know?"

"I hope not. When was the last time you talked with Rosa?"

"I ran into her a couple of years ago at the grocery store, and we talked about ten minutes in the middle of the aisle. We both agreed we should get together sometime, but neither of us followed through."

Except for the occasional sound of the wind, silence grew in the truck's cab as the minutes slowly ticked by. Leaves blew across the yard and down the drive, making the solitude seem to expand and take on a life of its own.

After ten minutes of waiting, Silas finally said, "Okay. Let's look around."

With her nerves on edge, she stepped out of the truck. See what they might learn from Rosa.

As the thoughts continued to swirl, nervous adrenaline pumped through her veins, causing her to take fast strides toward the home. Her running shoes disappeared in the tall grass. The front door was locked, and they walked around to the back.

"It's open," Silas said. Dust covered the furnishings, and a few leaves lay scattered on the floor. "Doesn't look like anyone has been out here in a long time."

A bad feeling continued to churn through her. *Please, God, let Rosa be okay.*

Their footsteps echoed on the tile floor as they walked through the deserted house. A door slammed in a back room. She whispered, "I don't like this. Empty houses give me the creeps."

"Most people feel that way."

"Yeah, well, count me in." After a look into the bedrooms, they retraced their steps through the living area into the connecting sunken den—a popular architectural feature of years gone by. Kennedy remembered this room was off-limits to the kids. The old pool table still stood in the center of the room, and an exquisitely carved bar sat on the far wall. Two leather chairs sat in front of a huge boxy television from in the days before flat screens became the thing.

She might feel a touch of sentimental reminiscing if it hadn't been for concern over Rosa not being here.

"Someone's been here recently."

Silas's voice made her jump, almost forgetting he was in the room. "What do you mean?"

He pointed. "The pool table is clean. Or at least the cue is." He picked up the long stick and inspected it before returning it to the felt. "And the counter. Fresh glass marks."

Circles the size of a glass or bottle marked a layer of dust on the bar. She watched as Silas strode behind the counter.

"Several bottles of wine are on the racks, and beer is in the refrigerator."

"What?" Kennedy hurried around the corner, and her gaze fell to the wine cooler and the mini fridge. Sure enough, it was stocked with beer. Two dirty wineglasses sat in the small sink. "Someone's been here."

"I'm assuming Winsett still owns this place."

"Yeah, as far as I know. To my memory, I never saw him drink beer, but kids don't always know what goes on with adults. He might not have done so in front of Rosa and me."

"True." Silas walked around the room, taking his time.

"I'm going to look at the bedrooms again." Kennedy hurried to the back of the house. Since it was a lake house, the furnishings were scarce and personal keepsakes nonexistent.

White bunk beds stripped down to the mattress were in the room she and Rosa slept in. Folded sheets were stacked high on the closet shelf. The main bedroom also had no sheets, but several blankets were piled in the corner. Kennedy picked up the top quilt and noticed a purple stain. Lifting it to her nose, she inhaled. Wine.

"Did you find anything else?" Silas stood in the doorway.

"Not really."

"What is it?" he asked.

She looked at him.

"Something's bothering you."

She sighed. "I guess I'm obvious. Has someone been sleeping here? I'm not certain, but I think that's a wine stain on that blanket." She pointed. "The cream-colored one. Or maybe I'm just surmising since it looks like someone's been drinking."

Silas simply stared at her but didn't respond.

Could he read her mind? Was it possible Glen came by to drink and maybe meet someone? Like a woman? Okay. Now she was being silly. The man she knew at the adoption agency was a family man. Not a sneak-off-to-the-lakehouse-for-an-affair type of man.

After a walk-through of the kitchen and utility room, they headed back outside. Silas checked his phone. "We'll give it ten more minutes, and then we're gone."

"Can we check out the boathouse? Rosa and I used to play up there." The metal building had a slanted roof that was low to the ground on the back side and high on the side that faced the lake. Iron balusters formed a miniature balcony with room for two chairs. The bare limbs of a huge pecan tree made it difficult to see the structure. She hoped it was too late in the year for snakes.

He started that way. "That doesn't sound like a safe place for kids."

She smiled. "We liked to sit on the roof and

look at the lake or play in the boat and pretend we were driving on the ocean and diving for sunken treasure." At his funny grin, she added, "We read a lot of adventure books, and the place was well cared for back then."

Silas opened the metal door, and she was careful to stand back. With his hand on the butt of his gun, he stepped in. After a second, he said, "Clear."

The mossy aroma assaulted her senses, and a chilly breeze blew, making the tin creak. An old fishing boat bobbed in the water. If the craft ever had a motor, it was long gone now. A dirt bike leaned against the side wall.

"Nothing." He glanced back out the open doors and stepped out.

She followed his direction. "Okay. I guess we can go. Looks like Rosa's not going to show. At least the text wasn't a setup."

The words were no more out of her mouth than a loud popping from the woods had her flinching. Bullets peppered the rickety building.

"Go! Go!" Silas shoved her back into the boathouse.

She squealed as the gunfire ripped through the tin walls.

Silas glanced from the boat to the motorcycle. As another bullet ricocheted in the shed, he jumped on the bike and jammed his boot down on the kick-starter four times before the engine sputtered to life. "Get on."

She took a step back. The thing didn't look big enough for the two of them. "You have a gun. Are we better off shooting our way out? Or wait on Randolph?"

Pounding on the tin above them had them looking up.

"They're in here." The male voice sounded from the roof above them.

"Never mind." She climbed on and wrapped her arms around his waist. "Go!"

Silas hit the gas, and the bike crashed through the door and raced across the yard as dirt kicked up around them.

"Stay down!" he yelled over his shoulder.

Limbs of a willow tree hung low, brushing across her back as she ducked as far down as possible. She squeezed her eyes shut as they sped across the rough terrain, bouncing and jarring with every dip.

The dirt bike felt like it might crumble under the weight of two people. She wished she were back on the ATV.

A barbwire fence separated the pasture on their left from the lake. Silas kept close to the shore and used the trees for protection. The lake was privately owned and only forty acres.

Large for someone's recreation, but small if someone was shooting at you.

No sooner had Kennedy begun to breathe again than she saw a blue truck barreling in their direction from the corner of her eye. She pointed. "Watch out!"

Silas maneuvered a sharp turn and bounded closer to the shore.

A man with dark hair and sunglasses sat behind the wheel. The truck gained on them.

Terraces stretched out in front of them. Silas gassed it and hollered, "Hang on."

All of her muscles tightened as the bike hit the steep slope and went airborne. She came off the seat and held on to Silas. They landed with a painful jolt that made her head snap forward. The back tire slid around to the right and the bike leaned to the left. Silas's knee hit the ground, and even while sliding sideways, he was able to get the machine back under control. He gave it full throttle.

Kennedy twisted and looked back in time to see the truck hit the terrace and soar through the air. The vehicle slammed into the ground before bouncing across the land, sending mud flying.

The trees grew dense in front of them. The vegetation looked too thick to penetrate. She prayed they could make it. The path narrowed between two oak trees.

"Take this." He held his Glock over his shoulder.

She took it and glanced back over her shoulder. The truck was mere inches from the bike. Every muscle in her body tensed as she squeezed the trigger. Again and again.

The truck's windshield shattered.

Her arm shook with every move of the bike, making her aim off.

The man ducked as the vehicle ran over a fallen log and soared through the air. It crashed into a tree and landed on its side.

Silas weaved through the woods, running over saplings and limbs before coming to a clearing. He slowed to a stop. "Good shooting."

"Thanks."

The woods blocked the wreckage from being visible. She wanted the man out of commission but didn't want to kill him. She'd never shot at anyone before.

"What's on the other side of the lake?"

"I don't know."

He glanced over his shoulder. "Can you look it up on GPS on your phone?"

"Sure." She pulled her phone out of her pocket, glad to once again escape the attack. If it hadn't been for Silas, there's no telling what she would've done. "When we get out of here, I want to check on Rosa."

"Randolph can do that."

After she punched in the address, she stared at the satellite map. "There's nothing out here except for a house to the left. That way." She pointed to the west.

"Okay." He put the bike into gear.

Putter. Putter. The engine died.

He removed the cap on the gas tank. "Out of gas."

Things just continued to get worse.

ELEVEN

Silas couldn't believe they were out of gas. At least the dirt bike had gotten them away from those guys first. "Let's leave this here and head to the house you saw on GPS."

"Gladly." Kennedy stretched and shoved her hands into the small of her back after she climbed off the bike. She bent at the waist to the right and then to the left. "My muscles are already paying for that wild ride."

"I imagine they are. Feels like a couple of those hits gave me whiplash."

"Exactly."

"Come on. I don't want to give those guys time to track us down."

Kennedy followed behind him through the brush. "I agree."

He withdrew his phone from his pocket and called Randolph. "Plans have changed. We were chased through the woods and are headed… Hold on—" He scrolled through his phone to the map and gave him the address. "Can you come pick us up there?"

"Yeah. Wait. I think I just passed it. I'm here."

"Wait on us. Looks like about a half of a mile hike through the woods." Silas explained about the guys who fired shots and chased them in the truck.

"Was it the same truck that was at Barclay's house?"

"No. This was a blue Ford with big tires." He held back the branches of a cedar tree to allow Kennedy to pass. "I'm not sure how many people are in on the attacks, but I think there's been at least three. More if there's a guy at the top calling the shots."

"I agree."

"I'm going to let you go. Talk in a bit." Silas clicked off.

Kennedy glanced back at the way they'd just come.

"I don't think they'll pursue us on foot, but let's not slow down to find out."

She picked up the pace. "I agree."

Fifteen minutes later, his legs burned, and he was sweating even in the forty-degree weather.

Kennedy had slowed, and occasionally let out a groan if a thorn got her. "It doesn't look like anyone is home."

Silas glanced at the property, taking in the brick home, the deck that crossed the back of the house, storage buildings, and what looked to be a pavilion for entertaining. An older boat sat under a cheap boat cover. A chain-link fence surrounded the perimeter, and a lock secured the gate. It wasn't a fancy place but still made a great getaway.

She shook and crossed her arms in front of her chest. "I'd suspect this was a lake house that is only used occasionally."

"I agree. There's Randolph's truck."

"Good. I'm ready to get out of here."

Silas helped her across the chain-link fence.

"That took a while," Randolph said as they drew near.

Kennedy glared. "It was a long hike. I'm tired of being chased and shot at. If I take a little time to slog through the woods, I'm fine."

Randolph threw his hands in the air. "I meant no insult."

Silas chuckled. With a twig dangling from her hair and mud smeared across her cheek, Kennedy looked beat. "We're both exhausted."

The other Ranger had the sense to nod in agreement.

After they all climbed in the truck, Silas said, "Head back to the lake house. Let's see if our boys are still there."

Randolph followed his directions around the dirt road, but when they got there, the blue Ford truck and the men were gone.

Silas took in the surroundings one more time. "I didn't figure they'd be here. My truck looks untouched. Let me check it out." He jogged to his truck and started the engine to let it warm. He gave Randolph a thumbs-up.

A few minutes later, he and Kennedy were back on the road again. Her head fell against the passenger window. "I'm so tired of this game. What's the plan now?"

He glanced at her. "I want to make it to the adoption agency before they go home for the day."

She sat straight in her seat. "We should have time. Uncle Glen, I mean Glen, stays late many nights. You know he's not really my uncle. All the kids that come through the agency call him that. Calling him by a family name made me feel like were kin, a close-knit group that could lean on one another. As much as I don't like to admit it, I do think he may have something to hide."

It brought no joy to hear the admission. "I agree. The Texas Rangers could obtain a search warrant, but it'd be easier if we had direct evidence. So far, it's circumstantial. Help me out. Tell me everything you know about the agency. Your mom's involvement. Glen. His family. How it works."

"Oh wow. That's asking a lot. After volunteering for the adoption agency, Mom went to work for them part time when I started private school in seventh grade. When I was little, I accompanied her to the office, and that's how I developed interest in troubled kids."

"The kids at the adoption agency are troubled? Aren't most infants?"

She waved her hand back and forth, indicating some. "A lot are. Occasionally, they'll work with the state or one of the local churches, where older kids are placed. Sometimes neglect or abuse is involved. And even though many of the children are small, neglect can affect even the youngest ones. Often, we don't know the extent of the damage until the kids are in our care and the truth comes out."

Silas turned onto the main highway as he considered this. He'd been asking himself how Harper could've wound up with the agency. "And are children ever suspected to be the result of kidnapping or human trafficking?"

"No. Not that I've heard. The state is strict with adoption agencies to make certain everything is legal. By what I know, Loving Heart Adoption Agency takes their role very serious. That's why I'm struggling."

"What leads you to believe they take it seriously?" He didn't want to put her on the defensive, but he wondered if she just liked the owner and his family, or if she had direct knowledge.

She fell silent for a second, as in thought. "Everything I know is secondhand. It's not like I worked at the agency or that Bring the Children Home Project deals with adoption agencies. Francis, the secretary, frequently answered calls where people wanted to know about the process of adopting, or if they wanted to give up a child, like the fees and the legal ramifications. Things like if they adopted and the biological parents change their minds, would the adoptive parents have any recourse."

"Sounds like reasonable questions." Silas braked as they entered the edge of Liberty. He couldn't wait to get a vibe for the organization. Even though he was almost positive the attacks involved the adoption agency, it was possible the lady who kidnapped Harper had plans for the child, but something thwarted her plans, and the woman dropped the toddler off at the agency.

Kennedy continued answering the question. "The agency used a law firm to handle its legal work. The firm was consulted every step of the way, which is one of the reasons private adoptions are so expensive." Kennedy seemed to relax the longer she talked. "I don't have experience with any other adoption agency, but I've heard few complaints."

As they neared the agency, he noticed it sat in a nice part of town. Silas had driven by the building a few times but had never paid it any attention. With well-manicured landscaping and large glass windows, it blended well with brick-and-stone buildings of lawyer's offices and investment firms.

He pulled into the concrete lot and parked on the side of the building behind a trimmed row of hedges. Five vehicles sat in the lot, all cars. Not that he expected to see one of the trucks the gunmen had used, but he'd been keeping his eyes open. He noticed Kennedy glance to the cars also. "Any of these belong to Winsett?"

"I don't know what he drives. He trades them often."

Silas opened the door for her as they entered the building. A desk sat in the middle of the room with a sign-in book.

"I'll be right with you," a female voice called from the back.

Seconds later, a lady dressed in a black business skirt with a cream silk blouse emerged. "Kennedy Wells, how are you?" The fortyish woman greeted her with a warm smile. "It's been a long time."

"Hello, Francis. It's good to see you." Kennedy shook her outstretched hand.

"Thanks." The woman glanced from her to Silas, her gaze briefly landing on his ring finger. "What can I help you with today? You're looking to adopt?"

Kennedy blushed. "No. I was wondering if Glen was in." It was a little awkward to call him uncle now that she was an adult but referring to him as Mr. Winsett or simply Glen didn't feel right either.

"No, he stepped out for a meeting, but I'm expecting him back shortly if you want to wait."

"Yes. Do you mind if I look around, especially at the playroom?"

The secretary looked a tad puzzled, but said, "Sure. You know your way around."

As they headed down the wooden floor of the hall, Silas asked, "How long has it been?"

"A couple of years, but more like six or seven since I volunteered. After I graduated from high school and started college, I've only dropped by occasionally. And once Mom got sick…"

"I understand."

Silas watched Kennedy as she took in her surroundings. What was going on in her mind? Was she suspicious of the agency owner, or was she building a defense? She stepped into the room on the right.

The room was bright and open. Miniature building blocks were stacked on a table, and a colorful rug lay on the wood-looking tile floor. Three beanbag chairs sat next to full shelves stacked with books and board games. Some kind of video game was connected to a small television. A plastic child-size kitchen filled another corner. A box in the shape of a caboose overflowed with dolls, trucks, balls and a variety of other toys.

Kennedy smiled. "Almost nothing has changed. Well, the toys are newer, but Rosa and I used to sit in beanbag chairs and read and visit for hours. Rosa could read faster than me, but we loved to share in the adventure. Oh." She plucked a book off the shelf. "These were my favorite mystery series. Teenage detectives who always solved the case."

"She was your best friend?"

Kennedy's face fell a tad. "Actually, Rosa was one of my only friends. I already told you, I was homeschooled. For two years, Mom put me in a coalition with other homeschooled kids, but then we got less active as time went on and finally dropped out until my parents enrolled me in private school in junior high. I always felt bad because I know it was difficult for my dad to pay the tuition, but somehow, he managed. I finished at the top of my class and got a full scholarship to college."

Silas could believe she had done well in school. He envied the way she talked about her parents. He could sense they had been close. But had her parents kept her at home because it was what they felt was best, or were they afraid someone would recognize she was Harper? If they had simply adopted her, why hide her away?

A door banged shut, and Kennedy turned to footsteps down the hall.

Francis held up a finger as she whisked by the open door. "Wait, that might be him."

A few seconds later, a voice boomed, "Kennedy Wells, get yourself back here." An older man with gray hair and a slight pudge around his belly strode into the playroom. Wrinkles creased his expensive dress shirt, and his tie hung loosely around his neck, giving the man a casual look.

The man barely glanced Silas's way.

Silas always had a way of reading people, and his gut told him Mr. Winsett already knew he and Kennedy were here waiting to talk with him.

"Uncle Glen." Kennedy smiled as the man embraced her in a big hug. She tried not to stiffen but didn't know if she succeeded. It felt awkward calling him uncle. She should probably drop the endearment.

"It's been too long." He turned to Silas, and his gaze lingered on his badge. "Who is your friend?"

"This is Texas Ranger Silas Boone. We wanted to visit with you."

"Sure, come on back to my office. Would you like a soda or coffee?"

They both shook their heads and followed the agency owner down the hall and past a conference-type room.

She and Silas sat in the leather chairs across the desk.

Glen shot them a seemingly genuine smile. "What can I do for you, Kennedy? You're not getting married, are you?"

"No," she said with a slight laugh, and felt heat come to her cheeks.

A smile spread across the man's face. "I thought maybe you were considering adoption."

"No…" She didn't glance at Silas to get his reaction.

"How is your father?" Glen leaned back in his chair and crossed his hands over his belly. "I know it must be difficult since he lost your mother. Your parents mean the world to me and Cora."

"Daddy's doing okay, considering." She tried to school her expression not to show too much emotion that might encourage more questions. "I came to ask you about my adoption."

If it weren't for the rapid blink of his eyes, Kennedy might've believed the question didn't surprise him.

"Adoption?" He leaned forward in his chair. "Who told you this, honey?"

"No one. I found the receipt in Daddy's office." The words felt strange as she said them. Receipt like a bill of sale. She couldn't go there, to the betrayal that kept threatening to bubble up.

Glen relaxed a little, and his eyebrows drew in as if forcing himself to be concerned. "Have you talked with your dad about this?"

Her heart raced, as she hated to be questioned like she was a child. "No."

"Ah. Well. You need to talk to Verne. I'm certain he can straighten everything out."

Straighten everything out. What did that even mean? Irritation crawled over her. She'd always loved and respected the fatherly figure sitting across from her, but now she detected insincerity in his demeanor. Her fingers played with the hem of her shirt, and she forced herself to stop.

"Mr. Winsett, there is no question about *if*

Kennedy is adopted. I've seen the documents."
Silas took over the conversation, for which she
was grateful. This was all too personal, making her hesitate to delve into the details. It was
quite different from helping others with their
problems.

A slight sound of movement by the door
caught Kennedy's attention. She turned to see
a tall young man with light sandy hair in the
doorway. Dressed in black skinny jeans, a pink
plaid dress shirt and tie, and a dark navy blazer
with tennis shoes, she guessed the guy might
work here. Wait. She'd seen the man before.
That was Rosa's husband, Colton. Kennedy
didn't think she'd ever get used to seeing men
wearing tennis shoes with business attire, but
maybe that was because she preferred men in
boots and jeans.

Colton's gaze stayed on Kennedy for several
moments before he caught Glen's questioning
glare and moved away from the door.

Glen's eyes narrowed at Silas. "I'm not at liberty to discuss Kennedy's care as a child." He
turned his attention back to her. "You should
know most of the rules about closed adoptions
simply by being here with your mother."

"Kennedy has been attacked multiple times,
as well as Elizabeth Barclay, the woman we believe to be Kennedy's biological mom." Silas

kept his tone even and noncombative, but his authority obvious.

She watched Glen for a sign of guilt, but the man was good at controlling his facial features. Through her job of counseling, she had grown accustomed to reading people, but Glen was difficult to make out.

He turned his gaze on her, oozing with concern. "Is this true, Kennie?"

He hadn't called her by her nickname in years, catching her by surprise. Glen had been the only one to call her by it after she became a teen. "Yes. Two men tried to kill us today. I received a text from Rosa to meet her at the lake house, but when we showed up, the men shot at us and tried to run us over in their truck."

"At *my* lake house?" Glen pressed his hand against his chest.

Was the man sincere, or a terrific actor? "Yes. Why would Rosa text me?"

"Rosa hasn't mentioned you in years. I have no idea why she would do that out of the blue. Were you injured? Do you need help?"

Silas said, "What we need are answers."

"You said this other lady was Kennedy's mom. I have no idea what or who you're talking about." Glen's face grew red. "Most of our adoptions are closed, which means you'd need a court order to open them."

Kennedy couldn't believe he was hiding behind the courts. Not in her case, anyway. Was this really the same man her family used to spend so much time with—a rock in her childhood? "Why are you doing this? Rosa and I were good friends. My mom volunteered for years for you. Our family and yours were close…"

Silas's hand reached out and squeezed hers, telling her it would be all right. He turned to Glen. "Is there anything you can tell us that would help us figure out who's behind these attacks? Someone kidnapped Elizabeth Barclay's child from a park. How did she wind up at your adoption agency?"

Glen got to his feet. "I have no idea what kidnapping you're talking about. This conversation is over." He turned his black eyes on Kennedy. "You need a court order to open adoption documents. Talk with your father. You and your family have been important to me and my family for many years. It rips my heart apart that you're going through this. But I can guarantee you, the Loving Heart Adoption Agency has nothing to do with any attacks."

Hurt assaulted her throat, and suddenly she wanted to cry. Glen knew more than he was saying. But why wouldn't anyone tell her the truth? This was her life, and she was in danger!

Silas got to his feet and held out a business

card. "Thank you for your help. If you think of anything that might be of benefit, please call."

"I will." Glen took the information and tossed it on his desk and followed them to the door.

Kennedy didn't say a word as suddenly she didn't know what to say. Francis gave them a wave as they walked down the hall, awkwardness filling the quiet of the soft footsteps on the floor.

Darkness had fallen and a chilly wind whipped across the parking lot by the time they walked to his truck. As soon as she slammed the door, Silas turned to her. "I'm sorry, Kennedy."

She glanced out the window, frustration eating at her. Who was she kidding? It was anger that stabbed at her heart. *Don't these people care?* Daddy and Glen. If Mama were still alive, would she, too, act like Kennedy had no right to answers?

"We didn't learn anything, but we're on the right track. I don't think Winsett will hand over evidence without a court order."

"You're right." Kennedy noticed movement behind the blinds in an office. If it were Glen, she couldn't tell.

"Did you notice the man in the aviator glasses that stopped outside the door?"

She nodded. "I did. That's Colton, Rosa's

husband. I've only met him once, back at their wedding."

"He works there?"

She shrugged. "Probably. It seems Rosa may've mentioned that."

"Okay. Back to the question at hand." Silas started the truck and pulled onto the street. "How did you wind up at an adoption agency?"

Her heart constricted. "Right. It's not probable someone took me for their own and then changed their mind, dropping me off at a safe place. How did a kidnapped child wind up being adopted? Is it possible Loving Heart Adoption Agency was the one behind the abduction from the beginning? Or was I *sold* to the agency?"

"Good questions."

But the big question lingered. Did her "adoptive" parents have something to do with it? The image of the receipt remained engrained in her mind.

My parents bought me.

Pain in her chest tightened, her world spinning out of control. The person or persons who had the most to lose would be who was behind the kidnapping. Right now, it seemed that could be someone she was close to. Someone she had trusted.

TWELVE

As Silas pulled out of the parking lot, he hit Randolph's number.

"What did you learn?"

"You're on speaker and Kennedy is with me." It was a longtime practice to let the other person know if anyone could hear their conversation. Silas gave him a rundown of the brief visit to see the owner of the agency.

"Sounds like either Winsett is our man, or he knows who is."

"That's what I think, too. Can you tail him for me? Our man got agitated toward the end of our conversation, and I'd like to see where he goes. Hopefully, we scared him enough to do something foolish."

"I look forward to it. But Boone, what about Kennedy?" Randolph cleared his throat like he was trying to keep the alarm from his voice. "If Winsett is our man, I don't think Kennedy should be anywhere near him."

Silas glanced her way. The streetlights reflected across the cab, and he noted her stiff posture. No doubt, she had the same concerns. He'd do anything to ease her fear. "I agree. I'll take her somewhere safe."

"Want to call the Jarvis County Sheriff's Department about Winsett?"

"I've already checked, and Winsett's home is in the county, so it's under their jurisdiction. I'll give the sheriff a call."

"Okay. I heard from Chasity at the office a few minutes ago on Victoria Rollins. Our victim had kidney failure and only months to live. She was taking dialysis three times a week. And get this." Randolph's tone grew more serious. "Twenty-four years ago, she and a man by the name of Arthur Westlake were arrested for attempted kidnapping in Dallas County. The case never went to trial due to a lack of evidence, so Victoria never saw the inside of a prison cell. No other arrests. But Arthur didn't learn his lesson. Three years later, hc robbed a convenience store, killed the clerk and is doing time in a Texas prison in Huntsville."

Silas let out a whistle. "Thanks for letting me know. What about financial records? Any ties between her and Winsett?"

"Not so far, but Chasity is checking into it."

"That's good news. Keep me informed if you learn anything more."

"I'll do it." As soon as Silas clicked off, Kennedy turned to him.

Her eyes sparkled. "You think Victoria Rollins may've been the lady who kidnapped me?"

"That's exactly what I think." Silas nodded. "And looking death in the face, she wanted to come clean."

A small smile crossed her lips. "That would make sense."

"One thing that bothers me."

Her smile faded. "What's that?"

"If you trust the memory of a nine-year-old boy, the lady I saw kidnap you threw you into the van and took off immediately, like someone else was behind the wheel. I didn't see the accomplice, but it's apparent Victoria didn't act alone. I'm going to assume the other person was Arthur, but it may've been someone else."

"I trust you. Even when you were nine."

Silas did a double take. The words shouldn't have pleased him, but they did. His headlights reflected off the pavement, and traffic picked up, everyone hurrying home to supper.

Colton, the man he'd seen at the adoption agency, kept returning to his mind. He was much too young to have been involved in the kidnapping, but something about him bothered

Silas. Like the way he stood at the door made Silas wonder if he'd been eavesdropping. "Do you know where Rosa lives?"

"I've got her address on my phone. Hold on." She scrolled through her contact list. "Here it is: 381 Sycamore Street in the Stone Creek neighborhood. Did you think Glen's reaction to Rosa texting me to meet him at the lake house was legit?"

"I know that area. Winsett seemed more interested where the meeting was supposed to take place than Rosa texting you."

"Right. Are we going to see her? It's already dark."

"Yeah, but it's only six thirty. That should give Colton time to get home. Are you up for it?" He glanced her way.

She nodded. "Yeah. I'm worried about her. Rosa wasn't the one who contacted me, but I don't want more people to get hurt. I'll feel better once I see she's all right."

Dread fell over Silas as he considered the next few hours. They were closing in on the perpetrator, but that would also pressure the guy to make a move—like cornering a wild animal while holding a big stick. The animal could turn tail and run or viciously attack and take you out. He and other law enforcement needed to be ready.

* * *

Kennedy closed her eyes and sighed in anticipation as Silas hit the doorbell—one of those equipped with a camera—on Rosa's upscale house. Streetlights and solar landscaping lights illuminated the area. Clear Christmas lights outlined the roof and a large wreath hung on the door. *Lord, please let my friend be safe. I don't want anyone else to be hurt because of me.*

Noise sounded from inside before the door cracked open a foot. Rosa stuck her face in the opening. "Yes?"

Relief that her friend was safe eased the weight on Kennedy's shoulders, but concern took its place. "Rosa? It's me. Kennedy."

A frowned lined Rosa's mouth. Her friend had always been an intelligent, caring person, and Kennedy instantly knew something wasn't right. "Hello. I hope we didn't come at a bad time, but we need to speak with you."

Rosa's dark eyes landed on Silas behind her. "I'm a little busy. Do you think you could come back another day?"

"Not really. We won't stay long. I promise."

"Who is it?" The door jerked back from Rosa's grip, and Colton stood there. His face burned red. "Kennedy and her Texas Ranger friend, correct?"

She swallowed down the lump that had suddenly formed. "Yes. It's been a while since we talked, and I didn't mean to ignore you at the agency." She waited, wondering if he would invite them in.

A baby cried from somewhere in the house, and Rosa said, "Excuse me. I must take care of Oliver."

Awkwardness hung in the air while Colton stared at Silas. Finally, he said, "Please, both of you come in."

Kennedy glanced back at Silas and caught his serious look before she followed Colton through the entryway into the all-white living room. Tall ceilings made the already large room feel enormous. Glass windows lined one wall, and decorative crown molding completed the rest of the room. A grand Christmas tree stood in front of the window with about five presents underneath. Kennedy wondered if there were anything in them, or if they were just for looks. A rock waterfall stood in the corner with soft a red light shining on it. The sound of running water should've been calming, but it made Kennedy's skin crawl. The decorations were simple, yet exquisite. Somehow, the fancy house didn't fit Rosa's sweet, down-to-earth personality. Or maybe Rosa had changed.

"Have a seat." Colton indicated the modern white sofa with metal legs.

Kennedy took a seat and immediately hated how the back of the couch came to her shoulder blades. Silas sat beside her, and his knees folded up high like he was sitting on a child's chair. If the situation weren't serious, it could've been humorous.

Rosa hesitantly stepped into the area carrying a small infant wrapped in a blue blanket. She sank onto a white wooden bench on the far side of the room.

Even though Kennedy had never received an invitation to a baby shower or a birth announcement, she said, "Congrats on the boy. I'm sorry for not reaching out until now."

Rosa smiled and then looked back down at the baby without a word.

Sadness seeped into Kennedy. What was wrong with her friend? Rosa had never been the loud partygoer, but quietly confident. A dependable friend whom everyone liked. To see her shrink—almost as in fear—broke Kennedy's heart.

Colton didn't glance his wife's way but gave his attention to Kennedy. "What can I do for you?"

What was she to do now? Talk to Rosa in front of Colton? Absolutely not. She preferred to talk to her friend alone. Colton held a smug, almost challenging expression. Like he dared Kennedy to confront him. She'd counseled these types of people in her job, and as always, she had to take a deep breath and not let her emotions rule. She hitched her chin a little higher and smiled. "This really has nothing to do with Colton, so I'd like to visit with Rosa alone. If you don't mind, gentlemen, could you give us some girl time alone?"

Silas climbed to his feet before she was through with the sentence. "Sure." He turned to Colton. "When we pulled up, I noticed you have a huge barbecue pit in the back. I've been thinking about buying a new one. Care to show me yours?"

"Certainly." He turned and gave Rosa a look. "We'll be out back, honey."

Silas flashed Kennedy a smile that said, *find out everything you can.*

As soon as the door shut, Kennedy moved over to Rosa. "Something's wrong. What is it?"

Rosa's gaze went to the door where Colton had exited. "Nothing. I'm okay. Probably just the baby blues."

She cocked her head at her friend. "Can I hold him?"

"Certainly."

Kennedy always felt clumsy holding a newborn, and she tried to keep the blanket wrapped snug around him as she cradled him in the crook of her arm. "He's perfect."

A smile tugged at Rosa's lips. "He is, isn't he?"

"Yes." Kennedy glanced toward the door and whispered in case Colton returned. She hated asking about Rosa's dad and his probable involvement, but she was afraid it'd make it worse if Colton overheard. "I received a text from someone claiming to be you asking me to meet you at your family's lake house. Was that you?"

"No." Rosa shook her head and concern etched her features.

"Silas and I were attacked. Shot at."

"Oh no." Her friend's hand went to her mouth. "Neither of you was hurt, were you?"

"Thankfully, no. I don't know if you've heard, but a couple of assailants have targeted us multiple times the last couple of days."

"I overheard Colton talking to my father on the phone about an attack, but I had no idea they were talking about you."

"Rosa," Kennedy leaned closer, careful not to disturb the baby. "Did you know I was adopted?"

"What? No." Her response sounded genuine.

"Through Loving Heart Adoption Agency."

Rosa frowned. "I didn't know. But you realize better than anyone that most of those are private adoptions."

"There's more. Not only was I adopted, but a lady kidnapped me from a park when I was three. My true mom is a woman named Elizabeth Barclay."

"What?" Rosa's dark eyes grew large. "Kidnapped? You must be mistaken."

"I wish I were. The Texas Rangers are investigating the cold case. They believe the attacks and my kidnapping are connected."

"How did you learn about your adoption? From your dad? Or did your mom tell you before she died?"

A knife to the heart made Kennedy's breath hitch. She wished her mom had been the one to tell her. She scooted closer to her friend. "Two days ago, I received a file—"

Rosa's gaze went over Kennedy's head.

She turned. Colton stood behind Kennedy. "Where's Silas? Is he salivating over your barbecue pit?" Okay, that didn't sound natural to her own ears. Oliver wiggled in her arms. She laid him on her shoulder and gently patted his back.

Rosa's husband, in his skinny jeans and tennis shoes, came to tower over them—an aggressive move to put them in their place. "What were you talking about?"

Rosa hurried to say, "About Oliver. Kennedy and I used to see each other a lot at the adoption agency. Who would've thought that we'd be the ones having babies now? Well, not Kennedy, but me." She held out her hands to Kennedy. "I'll take him now. Your arm must be falling asleep."

Silas quietly moved beside Kennedy as she handed the baby off and stood. "It was nice meeting you, ma'am."

Rosa pulled the baby close to her breast. "Oliver is hungry. I'm going to the nursery to feed him. It was nice of you to stop by." Without as much as a glance, she hurried from the room.

Silas moved toward the door. "We better be going. I appreciate your time."

Kennedy could feel Colton's eyes on her as she walked out of the house and down the sidewalk. Even once they were in the truck, they remained silent until they pulled out of the drive and onto the highway.

"Did you learn anything?" Silas asked.

"Not much, except she claims she didn't know my parents adopted me. Going by the expression on her face, I'd say she was telling the truth. She wanted to know how I had learned about the adoption."

"What about the text?"

"She didn't send it." Kennedy was relieved Rosa hadn't been in trouble, but that begged the question of who sent the text.

"That's what I figured." He glanced her way. "Did you ask her about her dad?"

She shook her head. "Not really. She reminded me that most adoptions were private. I was just about to tell her about the file and the attack when Colton came in." A strange feeling in her stomach churned. "Did you feel Rosa was scared to speak? Especially in front of her husband?"

"That's putting it mildly. Has Rosa always been the timid sort?"

"Quiet, but not timid. As adults, we haven't spent much time with each other, so she might have changed. I was wondering if she and Colton had been fighting."

"The tension was obvious, so it's possible."

"Okay. So it's not just me." What if Rosa knew about the adoption, and her daddy was involved? Would Rosa defend him? Protect him? She had Oliver to consider now. Colton worked for her father.

Kennedy liked most people and gave them the benefit of the doubt, but there was something about Rosa's husband she didn't like. Not only did he seem unconcerned about his wife, but the baby as well.

Now that she had time to think about it, concern for Rosa's safety grew. What had happened to make her a nervous person? Was Rosa truly surprised by the news Kennedy was adopted? Or had she, too, known all along?

THIRTEEN

Rain hit the windshield, and Silas continued driving down the rough Texas country roads. He checked his rearview mirror to make certain they weren't being followed. Not another vehicle in sight. They'd left Rosa's house over an hour ago and had stopped by a convenience store for a few groceries. He hated to drive this far away from the hospital and his home, but he knew Kennedy would be safer away from the gunmen until they knew who was behind the attacks.

Liz had called to say she might be released from the hospital tomorrow. He was glad she was feeling better, but he worried about her being at her home alone. The hospital would offer her better protection for unwanted visitors. Anyone who attacked her there would have plenty of witnesses.

The road turned sharply, and he slowed. No one knew about his connection to this place in the boonies that his granddaddy used to farm. It'd been over twelve years since Silas had been there. Because of the thick woods, it'd be almost impossible to find by accident.

He glanced at Kennedy. She was curled halfway on her side, her head against the passenger door and his leather coat wrapped around her. His protective instincts kicked in. Safe. He needed to keep her secure. Something he hadn't been able to do before, but he was no longer a nine-year-old kid.

No matter how many times he tried to remember the specifics of the kidnapping, there were only the same old details. Harper climbing the steps up the ladder as he slid down. When he told her to wait on him, she yelled, "I can do it myself."

He thought it was funny and teased her he was coming to get her, so she better hurry.

A car door slammed.

He climbed the ladder as Harper giggled and slid down. When he got to the top, he saw a lady in a red coat hurry toward the slide, and Silas realized something wasn't right. He heaved himself down the plastic tunnel, but when he came out the other end, Harper screamed for the lady to put her down.

His feet hit the dirt, and he sprinted after the lady in the red coat, yelling for her to stop.

Harper screamed and held her hands out to Silas. The woman shoved her into the open side door of the van, and its tires squealed as it took off.

Silas chased the van as the taillights disappeared around the corner. He continued running, huffing and puffing, even when the van was out of sight, until he made it to the end of the block.

Someone else was driving the van. But who? Glen Winsett or someone else? Victoria Rollins was dead. What had happened to the driver?

Another sharp turn appeared before he slowed and eased through the curve. The entrance should be right here. Hidden among the dead grass, he spotted the sagging barbwire gate and turned in. It only took a moment for him to pull into the drive and shut the gate again.

"We're here?" Kennedy sat up straight and rubbed her eyes.

"Yeah."

"Did I fall asleep?"

He smiled. "As soon as we hit the road."

She frowned. "I must've been exhausted. I didn't snore or anything embarrassing?"

"No." He chuckled. "I'm sure you needed the rest." The road dipped to the right and a huge mudhole appeared in the headlight beams. He gassed it and plowed through, sliding to solid ground.

They entered the dark shadows of the trees, being swallowed up. She said, "Are you certain there's really a house back here?"

"A house might be an exaggeration. More like a shack. But there's electricity, and indoor restroom facilities."

"I believe in counting my blessings."

A few saplings had grown in the dirt path, and he ran them over. A temporary creek ran through the drive, and he hit the gas. When he reached the water and his truck sank, he pressed the accelerator. The tires sank deeper.

Kennedy remained silent as she stared out the window, and her hand gripped the handle for support.

He put it in Reverse, trying to back up, but the tires spun. Then forward again. Three times of rocking the truck back and forth, his tires found traction, and going sideways advanced to the other side. "That was close."

"Yeah. Hopefully, we'll be able to get out in the morning."

Silas had the same thought. But at least that meant anyone else would also have a hard time making it up the drive. A small clearing appeared, and the headlights shone on the small shack. It was worse than he remembered, and he prayed the electricity was still in working order.

If Kennedy had more doubts, she didn't say so.

"Let me make certain it's safe to enter."

"Okay. Be careful."

He shrugged into his slicker, stuffed his flashlight into a pocket and pulled his Stetson on his head. "I'll be right back."

Rained pelted him as he jogged through the puddles to the door. There wasn't a porch or protective cover, so he just shoved the door open. After a moment's pause to make certain no animal or person jumped out, he flipped on the light switch. Besides multiple old dirt dauber nests and evidence of rodents, the place wasn't as bad as what he imagined.

He hurried back to the passenger side of the truck and opened the door. He took off his slicker and put it over her. "Come on. I think we're good."

"Brr. It's freezing out here." She pulled the slicker over his jacket, thankful to stay dry, and dashed for the door.

A pile of old logs leaned against the wood-burning stove. "Looks like it's been years since anyone has been here, but the rule has always been to restock the wood before you leave. Let me see if I can get this going."

Kennedy walked through the house, evidently checking it out.

The logs were well seasoned, and with the help of a fire starter and an old newspaper, he had a blaze going almost instantly. The paper was dated seven years prior, so he assumed the place been empty that long.

Suddenly a swishing sound had him turning, and he saw Kennedy was making herself busy with a broom.

"It's not as bad as what I had envisioned, but I would feel better if the floor were clear of debris." A large drop of water pinged her on the head, and she looked up. "I spoke too soon."

"Let me get a pan or bucket." He found an old coffee can with a few nuts, bolts and coins in it. He emptied it on the counter and then hurried to put it under the leak.

Twenty minutes later, Kennedy had the floor swept and the counters washed. Silas grabbed sheets and blankets from the chest. He shook them out to make certain there were no insects or reptiles that had sought refuge in the warm environment. One blanket was eaten with mole holes, and he returned it to the chest.

He sent Randolph a text to let him know they made it to the cabin.

"Whew. I don't know if the fire has taken the chill off or because I'm working, but I already feel warmer." Kennedy sat on the couch that she'd already dusted.

"Probably a little of both. The house is not that big, so it warms quickly. I don't think we were followed, but I'm going to check around outside."

"Okay."

Was that nervousness he detected in her tone? He had hoped Kennedy would feel better being farther away from the danger, but maybe being secluded worried her more. Both of their houses would be the first place an attacker would look for them. Randolph traded off with Dryden at the hospital while Dryden went to a hotel to sleep.

Silas gave her one last glance before heading back outside with his hat and slicker. The rain had slacked to a drizzle, but with all the moisture, every little bit made the ground muddier and more miserable.

Darkness engulfed the woods, the silhouettes of the trees coming together to form a black mass. Someone could stand ten feet away, and you wouldn't be able to see them. He pulled his slicker closed, readied his gun and stepped into the rain. His boots made a sucking sound with each step.

The wind had died down. He moved around the corner of the house, and his eyes adjusted to the darkness. Little could be seen. The flashlight would make him an obvious target.

Wet leaves covered the ground along with muddy bare spots. He stepped lightly and moved away from the house. The only thing visible from the woods was the rickety cabin. Not only did a glow come from the windows, but the smoke from the chimney lingered in the air. He hoped the trees would sift the odor should someone come along, making their location difficult to determine. A huge cedar with a broken limb made a great place to stand and observe.

An engine hummed somewhere in the distance. He listened, trying to determine which direction it came from. After several minutes, the noise faded away.

Ten minutes passed, and then another. A couple of times he saw Kennedy's shadow in the window. She'd placed her trust in him, and he was determined not to let her down. Liz was healing and hopefully would be home tomorrow. Like he'd told Kennedy earlier, if Glen Winsett was their man, Silas had pushed his buttons and they'd needed to be prepared for more trouble.

As much as Silas had fought it, he had drawn closer to Kennedy. He'd failed her once, but maybe they could put all this behind them.

Time could not be turned back, but they could start where they were now.

Just like Silas and his dad? The thought came to him suddenly. No, their relationship was past the healing point. During Silas's teen years, they had typical father-son disagreements, but nothing compared to when he told his dad he wanted to be a Texas Ranger. His dad wanted him to be an engineer or get into business. In his twenties, Silas began to resent his father's criticism. As a kid, he'd spent a lot of summers with his grandparents on the farm, and they had instilled a respect for authority, including for his parents. He hung in there and tried to get along, until one Sunday afternoon he and his dad once again got into it. "Go on. Be a loser like your granddad and do nothing with your life. Get out of here and don't ever come back."

His mom had chased him to his truck, apologizing, but that had been the last straw. Granddad was Silas's hero. Silas hadn't visited his folks' house or talked with his dad in all these years.

Why was talking to his family so difficult? Was his dad so disappointed in Silas's career choice he didn't want to work things out? Or had he regretted the fight but was too stubborn to make the first move? What if Silas tried to make amends and his dad declares he doesn't want a relationship?

Silas didn't know if he could take the rejection. Sometimes things were better off left alone.

Movement to the right nabbed his attention, instantly bringing him out of his thoughts.

He gripped his pistol and stared into the darkness.

Drizzle continued, and the only sound was that of water dripping from the trees and hitting the ground.

A shadow moved by the corner of the house. "Silas..."

He released a pent-up breath.

"Are you out here?" Kennedy called a little louder.

Allowing his pistol to drop to his side, he hurried in her direction. "I'm right here."

"I worried about you, wondering if something had happened to you. Next time let me know if you plan to stay gone that long."

He wanted to tell her that she could've gotten hurt or blown his cover, but he kept his remarks to himself. She was right. He should've explained his intentions, so she'd know. "You're right. Next time I will."

She wrapped her harms around herself. "How much longer?"

It's a little late for that now. "I'm ready to come in."

As soon as the back door shut, they took off their shoes so as not to track mud through the house.

"I messed up by coming out there, didn't I?"

"I should've let you know my plans. My fault."

She let out an audible sigh. "Nice of you to say, but I knew better." She rubbed a hand across the back of her neck. "The thought even crossed my mind not to go out there just in case you had spotted someone. But then scenarios swirled of you being taken at gunpoint. I know better."

"Hey." He looked at her. "Cut yourself some slack. Don't be so hard on yourself."

She padded across the linoleum floor and flounced down on the old green leather couch. "I try not to be. I'm fighting with so many things right now. Tell me what you remember."

"About the kidnapping?" They had already gone over that, but maybe she needed to hear it again.

"No. My parents. Dax. Shasta. My dad. Mom. Anything and everything. I feel like I've lost a part of myself and can't get a grip on reality. My narrative has changed."

"Your narrative?"

She laughed. "I don't know what classes you took in college, but I'm sure you studied it. Never mind. Just tell me what you know about me."

That made sense to him. "Your mom, Liz, babysat me, but you already knew that. I really liked your mom." At her nod, he continued. "My mom and dad both worked, so I spent a lot of my time either at your house, or at my grandparents'."

"Do you resent them for that?"

"No." He grinned. "Should I lie on the couch?"

"Ha ha. No." Her lips turned up at the corners.

"I understood parents had to work, and they couldn't leave me alone. My grandparents taught me to work hard and were good to me. I spent a lot of my time on the farm and working outside. Your mom was the bake-cookies, let-a-kid-be-a-kid type of person." He smiled. "And what kid wouldn't enjoy running a Christmas tree farm?"

"That does sound like a fun treat." Kennedy's eyes sparkled. "Tell me about it."

"From the day after Thanksgiving until Christmas Eve at noon, they ran the business, offering hot chocolate or apple cider to their customers. Your dad put me to work."

"Doing what?" She pulled her feet on the couch and wrapped her arms around her knees.

"I helped with the planting in the spring. As I got older, I enjoyed using an ax to chop down the trees for customers."

"I guess it made you feel like a man?" Her eyes twinkled.

He laughed out loud. "I suppose it did. Some people like to cut their own, but if not, I did the honors. I got to show off. I'm sure people were just being nice, but someone would comment about the young strong man I was."

Kennedy giggled. "I can see you enjoyed it."

"I did. Those were good memories."

A smile developed, and she stared off at the stove. "Was there a tractor?"

"What?"

"A red tractor with lights that outlined the wheels. I don't know if I dreamed it, or if I have a memory."

Silas reached across the couch and pulled her hand into his. "Your dad owned a red Farmall tractor that he used to plow the tree field, but then he'd decorate it for Christmas every year. Kids used to get their picture made on it."

She turned to him. A grin came to her lips and her eyes glistened. "My daddy wore overalls and a brown cowboy hat."

"Yes, he did." Joy filled his heart. "You remember."

"I remember," she whispered.

Silas wrapped his arms around her into a hug and inhaled her coconut-scented shampoo. He soaked up her warmth as she melted in his arms. What was he doing? She was confused about who she was, and the last thing he needed was to disappoint someone else. He relaxed his arms and allowed them to drop beside him.

"What about me?" She coughed into her arm. "Did you have to tell me to get lost and quit bugging you?"

If she noticed the tension, he couldn't tell. He loved watching her reaction to hearing about her family. "You were ornery, but a good kid. I always had to keep an eye on you because you were self-sufficient. You wanted to do things for yourself, and the word *can't* wasn't in your vocabulary."

Her smile slowly faded. "I remember getting in a lot of trouble from my mom and dad for not doing as I was told. They constantly asked why I couldn't listen. Looking back, maybe because they knew I was kidnapped, I suppose they preferred I be quiet and not draw attention to myself. The more they tried to get me to listen, the more I rebelled. So much that they didn't put me in school until seventh grade. And even then, it was a small private school. I'm not complaining, but it fits together with the puzzle a little more. Dad made little money, and private school was expensive."

"It doesn't mean they had anything to do with your abduction."

"I agree." She shook her head and swiped at her eyes. "My eyes are itching. Must be the wood smoke. Please don't misunderstand. My parents were good folks and loved me very much."

Did she really believe that, or was she trying to convince herself?

Silas's eye burned, and he rubbed it. Realization hit him. Smoke. The cabin was filling with smoke.

Kennedy straightened. "The house is on fire! We've got to get out of here."

Silas jumped to his feet and warned, "Wait." Smoke bellowed from the wood-burning stove. "The cabin's not on fire. Someone's trying to smoke us out. They must've put something to block the chimney flue."

And as soon as one of them stepped out of the door, they'd be shot.

Kennedy held her breath, and her stomach swirled with nerves. She whispered, "Can we put out the fire?"

"I don't know." Silas coughed and held up the blanket that had fallen to the linoleum. "Lay down on the floor and cover your head with this."

She did as asked. The cold floor brought fresh air to her lungs.

She watched as Silas used his shirt to shield his face from the smoke and strode to the bedroom to crack open the window. Smoke billowed through the opening.

The lights flickered, and then the house plunged into darkness. Her grip on the blanket tightened. With the black iron encasing the wood-burning stove, only a sliver of light danced from the flames. They were trapped. How long did it take to die from asphyxiation? She didn't want to panic, but as her lungs struggled to get oxygen, she had the desire to run for it.

Silas knelt beside her and coughed. "Are you okay?"

"Yes. But I'm going to put the fire out." She jumped up from the floor and headed toward the kitchen. Her eyes burned.

"Don't do that. It'll only make it worse." A hand clamped down on her shoulder. "Come with me. We're getting out but stay together." He gagged. "Back door."

Without a word, he took her hand and rushed

toward the kitchen, feeling along the wall for orientation. She tried to inhale a deep breath, but it was no use. Her lungs simply couldn't take in air. The room swirled.

Silas jerked opened the door and smoke bellowed through the opening. They swiped their shoes by the door and quickly yanked them on.

Not concerned with being quiet, Kennedy staggered outside, Silas behind her. Both of them coughed and gagged.

Gunshots went off and bullets slammed into the side of the house. Silas took her hand and jogged along the side of the house to the back. She hunkered low. Why didn't they head to the truck?

No matter how much she concentrated, she couldn't keep from hacking. Her foot slid in the mud, but she kept going, using Silas for support. Mist hung in the air from the rain, making the ground tragically slick. As soon as they were under the cover of the trees, he stopped and looked back in the direction the shots were fired.

Reflection shone off Silas's truck, but if another vehicle parked close, Kennedy couldn't find it. The constant dripping of moisture from the leaves made it difficult to hear if anyone moved about.

He grabbed a stick from the ground and

chucked it toward the house. It landed with a thud. Gunfire went off again from the back side of the house.

Silas rapidly returned fire. "Run for the truck."

Her heart raced, and with shots being fired, she sprinted across the side yard. She couldn't tell which shots were from the assailant and which were from Silas, but she didn't wait around to find out. She jumped into the cab but stayed low.

A second later, the driver's-side door opened, and Silas slid in. He started the truck and flew backward, kicking up muck with the tires spinning.

She put on her seat belt and looked out the back window. "Tree!"

Too late. The back bumper slammed into the trunk, and her head snapped sideways. He shoved the gearshift into Drive and Low, hit the gas. Sludge splattered the windows.

The headlights cast an eerie glow on a man striding toward them with his gun aimed.

"Get down!" Silas shoved her head into the seat, and she dropped onto the floorboard. He leaned over the console but kept his foot on the accelerator. Going sideways, he gained traction through the grass. The truck bounced.

With the revving of the engine and gunfire,

it was impossible to tell what was going on, but the truck kept moving.

Silas slammed on the brake, and the truck slid to a stop.

She didn't know if it was safe to climb back into the seat or if she needed to stay down.

"Texas Ranger Silas Boone. Drop your weapon."

She peeked over the dash. The headlights shone on Silas with his Glock aimed at a man. The guy tossed his gun to the mud and put his hands in the air. Two minutes later, the man wore handcuffs and was sitting on the ground. Silas talked into his cell phone, but the words were too garbled to decipher.

The immediate danger seemed to be over, but her heart continued to thunder in her ears. She squinted to get a better look at the man. His dark clothes and scraggly hair made him look like a thug. Was he another hired man? Or the man behind the attacks?

The assaults needed to stop. But for the life of her, she didn't know what she could do. Sitting like a duck in the crosshairs of a hunter's gun was not helping.

FOURTEEN

Kennedy glanced up as Silas stepped into the room. They'd come back to his place last night after Randolph arrived, and the man at the cabin—Jose Martinez—was taken into custody. She'd grabbed a couple of hours of sleep, which was two more than Silas got.

Silas said, "Liz just called. She will be released this afternoon from the hospital."

"Oh, I'm so relieved." No sooner than the words were out, she changed her mind. "I worry about her safety. Will she be going to her house alone? Won't that put her in danger?"

"Dax and Shasta will be with her. Shasta will spend the night." Silas must've read the argument on Kennedy's face and held up his hand. "After we search Winsett's house, the Texas Rangers will watch over her."

She nodded. "Thank you. Now that I've met my *first* mom, I want nothing else to go wrong."

"The investigation continues to lead back to the adoption agency. Victoria Rollins worked for Winsett during the first year they were in business. And Winsett withdrew ten thousand dollars in cash from his bank account hours before you arrived at Liz's. Neither Lyle Baker nor Jose Martinez has a bank account, but it looks like Glen paid them."

Silas had already given her the update on Victoria over coffee and scrambled eggs this morning.

She glanced out the window. Only a few clouds lingered in the sky, and except for a few puddles, all signs of last night's rain were gone.

Her gaze turned back to Silas. He leaned against the door frame, his hand resting easily at his front pocket and his Stetson shoved back. She supposed he was waiting for her reply. "Besides the money, do you have more evidence against Glen?"

"Not specifically him, but the Loving Heart Adoption Agency. Kennedy, his hands have got to be dirty."

"The money could've been for something else. I have a real hard time believing he would try to kill me. But when all the evidence is produced, I'll trust the facts."

"We're getting a search warrant as we speak."

As if on cue, Silas's cell phone rang. "This

is Boone." The cowboy nodded as he listened. "I'll be right there."

After he clicked off, Kennedy leaned forward. "You got the search warrant?" At his nod, she climbed to her feet. "I'm ready."

He held his hand up. "You can't go into the Winsett home."

"You want me to stay here by myself? You had my car dropped off at my house."

"I wished I would've had it delivered here. I want you protected, and since Dryden and Randolph will be with me, you can come. But you'll have to stay in the truck."

Annoyance tugged at her, even though she knew he was right. She didn't know the rules, but she doubted the victim was supposed to search for evidence in the suspect's home.

They were quiet on the drive over, each in their own thoughts.

Forty minutes later, he turned into Rock Ledge Trail housing development. Water shot into the air from a fountain centered in the gorgeous lake and a waterwheel churned next to a massive red barn. Kennedy thought she'd like to get married in a barn. This one looked like the owners built it to imitate an old barn, but it had all the conveniences of new construction. Beautiful, costly homes sat on manicured lawns of over an acre.

Winsett's place was one of the first homes built in the development and encompassed more acreage. No other homes sat between it and the entrance. The image of the $30,000 receipt returned to her mind. How much money had Winsett made at the agency? CEOs or people who ran organizations normally made a decent income, but was it all legal? Did Glen realize she'd been kidnapped all these years, or was he also a victim? She liked to give people the benefit of the doubt.

If only she'd been a little older when she had been taken, maybe she'd be able to help with the investigation.

Silas drove down the concrete drive and pulled to the side of the house. No other vehicles sat parked outside. She said, "Doesn't look like Glen's home."

"I'm sure Winsett will be here soon. Ranger Randolph said to meet him here at ten o'clock."

The house was dark like no one was home, and Kennedy hoped his wife wasn't there. She could only imagine what the allegations would do to their family. Poor Rosa. Did Cora, Glen's wife, know what was going on? The whole family would be impacted.

Silas's cell phone rang again, and he answered. "Hold on." He held up his finger to Kennedy like he'd be right back and exited the truck. He strode underneath a huge pecan tree with the phone to his ear.

The sun broke through the clouds and shone into Kennedy's eyes. She wished he would've parked under the carport. Where did Silas go? He was no longer under the tree. Maybe he'd walked around the house to get a better signal.

Boom!

An explosion and orange flames whooshed, engulfing the house, and came near the truck.

Silas!

Flames shot high into the sky, and an enormous black cloud of smoke mushroomed, drowning out the sun. She jumped out of the truck and sprinted in the direction Silas had gone.

Silas found the truck's cab empty and ran around the side of the house, searching for Kennedy. Like an oven, heat encompassed him. He buried his face in his arm to block the smoke and searched the area. His lungs burned, and his eyes stung. "Kennedy!" On the ground, beside the tree, Kennedy's body lay face down.

"Are you all right?" He knelt beside her, his eyes taking in the embers on her back. He quickly flicked them away. "Kennedy?"

She slowly rolled and looked at him, her brown eyes wide.

"Are you okay?" he repeated.

"Yeah, I think so. After the explosion, I ran to see if you were okay, thinking you had gone in the backyard. Then there was a second blast. I really don't remember much except for being knocked to the ground." Suddenly, she turned and placed her hand on the ground, trying to get up. Gently, he helped her to her feet. She wavered and clutched her head. Without thinking, he scooped her into his arms, her head tucked under his chin. The odor of singed hair assaulted him. He carried her to the passenger side of his truck. The heat continued to swell. "Hold on."

He jogged around to the driver's side and drove the truck backward away from the house. Popping from minor explosions continued as more things gave way to the fire. He started to call it in, but he saw Ranger Randolph speed down the drive and pull in behind them.

Kennedy sat up straight and looked more aware than just minutes before.

Silas rolled down the window.

"What happened?" the Ranger asked.

"Had a little surprise for us."

"Anyone hurt?" His friend's gaze went over to Kennedy.

"I think we're fine," she said, but her voice

shook. No doubt the shock knocked her off-balance.

"Good." Randolph nodded with a smile.

Pop. Pop. Pop.

Gunfire sounded from the trees.

Pain lit Ranger Randolph's face as he jerked, clung to his chest and fell to the ground.

"Get down. Get down." But Kennedy had already sunk farther into the floorboard with fear in her eyes.

Silas quickly jumped out of the truck and covered his partner with his body.

Pop. Pop.

Bullets pinged the side of his truck and whizzed past his head. He had to get the Ranger to safety. The shooter moved, nabbing his attention. Silas withdrew his weapon and fired multiple times into the trees where he'd seen the gunman.

Keeping low, he opened the back door of the cab. "We're going to get you out of here."

Randolph clutched his chest area. He didn't say a word but let out a groan as Silas helped him onto his feet and into the vehicle. As soon as the Ranger was in, Silas hurried into the front seat, started the engine and jammed it into Reverse.

"Hang on." His truck shot backward around Randolph's truck, and when his tires swerved off the pavement, he whipped it around, shifted into Drive and took off.

"Where's backup? Shouldn't everyone else be here?" Kennedy asked.

"Should be here any minute." He tossed his cell phone to her. "Call Luke Dryden. His number is under Dryden." He would've thought they'd already be here, too. As he neared the area by the barn, there was more gunfire and his front passenger tire blew out, sending his truck out of control. The vehicle went to the right, into the man-made creek for the waterwheel. Rocks lined the ditch, sending his truck pitching before the wheel dug deep into the stream. The truck leaned forward and to the left. There was no way he could get it out now.

Kennedy sounded like she left Dryden a message on voice mail.

He could sit in the truck with Kennedy and Randolph and hope to hold off the gunmen. Or he and Kennedy could run for it, hoping to divert the attention away from the injured Ranger.

Two men weaved through the trees at a run.

Neither option avoided danger.

FIFTEEN

Kennedy's heart raced as she looked over the seat at Ranger Randolph. His pale face contorted into a grimace. "We have to get him help."

"No time," Silas pointed out. "The gunmen are headed our way. Come on. Now."

He didn't leave room for argument, but she made room anyway. "We can't leave him."

"Kennedy, if all three of us stay together, we make one target. I don't think Randolph is even their target, but he will be if he remains with us."

She didn't enjoy leaving the Ranger, but she saw Silas's point. Scrambling across the seat, she got out on the driver's side.

"Stay close," he said.

She had no intention of running her own way. He kept his gun ready but didn't shoot as they crossed the stream and then dashed for the barn. The ground was bare, and rocks littered the dirt.

More gunfire broke the silence, sending her heart into her throat. Bullets kicked up the soil all around them. Silas answered with several rounds. They hunkered behind the barn and made their way to the other side. A concrete sidewalk led to a side door, and a trash receptacle with a lid stood outside. The entrance appeared to be to a kitchen. Silas pulled on the handle, but it was locked.

As they continued around the side of the building, she prayed all the doors were not locked. But of course, they would be. This place was used for weddings. If only it were a real barn.

Her gaze kept returning to the trees and their surroundings. The gunfire had stopped, but no doubt the men hadn't left.

The next door they tried was locked as well, and then she spotted the stalls. "Come on. Over here."

Open stalls and hay piles lined the wall on the far side. A Texas longhorn lazily munched straw. Silas glanced at her before both of them moved toward the wooden ladder that led to the loft. Kennedy had never climbed so fast in her life. Silas was right behind her. The vast loft was the width of the entire building. She hurried across the wooden planks to the far end.

Hay and feed lay at the front and a variety

of wedding props littered the rest with only a narrow walkway down the middle. With Silas's hands on her back, urging her on, she moved all the way to the back corner behind a couple of white column-like sepulchers. Without a word, she sank to her knees, and Silas knelt beside her.

If the gunman climbed the loft, they'd be sitting ducks.

"Stay here."

Her hand shot out and grabbed his arm before he left. "Where are you going?"

"We can't sit here and wait. I need to keep watch on Randolph, but I don't want to worry about your safety. Stay hidden." He reached into his boot and withdrew a second gun, this one much smaller. "This is my .38. It's not big, but it can get the job done. Use it if you need to."

With that, he hurried down the aisle and then was gone. The creepy feeling of being alone didn't sit well with her. She heard his boots on the ladder and then silence.

She glanced around at all the furnishings, pleasant, pretty things that were used on the happiest day of someone's life. So much for that. She just hoped to make it out alive.

Several minutes passed with no discernible sounds of Silas or the gunmen. Occasionally, the cow moved down below her and once she heard the animal drink. The waiting made her antsy.

What really bothered her was she didn't hear any other vehicles pull down the drive. Had the other officers been notified about the explosion, and were they making their way across the property? Or had they been ambushed, and no one was coming? How was Ranger Randolph? Was he even still alive?

So many questions and no way to find answers sitting in this loft.

The temptation to climb down and see what was going on was great. She wasn't a gun expert and didn't know what kind the two gunmen carried, only that her gun was much smaller.

She wished she'd had taken classes from Annie Tillman, the team's weapon instructor. Better yet, she wished Annie were beside her. Counseling families was important for family victims to a child abduction, but Kennedy wished she had trained in other areas as well.

Two shots sounded in the distance.

She stiffened. *Please, Lord, be with Silas. Don't let him get shot. Or Randolph again.* Sinking to a sitting position, she wrapped her arms around her knees and tried to become as tiny as possible.

The sound of a rock skittering across the concrete snagged her attention, and her heart raced. Was someone down there?

She strained to listen, and then she heard it again. Footsteps. *Silas?* Surely he'd warn her if it were him. She slid the gun from her coat pocket. Was it ready to fire? Did it have a safety? Her daddy's shotgun was much easier to remember how to work.

A cow bawled. The longhorn.

Movement sounded below and then steps on the ladder.

Someone was climbing into the loft!

She clamped her eyes shut. *Please, Lord, protect me.*

Silently, she shifted even more behind the columns. A glance around gave her no ideas of escape. Her palms grew sweaty even as a cold breeze whipped through the rafters. She drew a deep breath, trying to calm her racing heart.

Heavy steps sounded on the wooden floor. Whoever it was, they weren't even trying to be quiet. She peeked around the column.

A tall man she didn't recognize strode down the aisle. Something fell, and she heard the sound of glass breaking. "I know you're in here. You might as well come out now."

She swallowed down the scream that threatened to escape. Even as she wondered if she could force herself to shoot another human being, the pistol grew cold in her grip as her finger tightened on the trigger. The steps grew closer. Using both hands, she raised the gun and waited.

Closer. Closer.

A long shadow passed over her. The man's eyes collided with hers, and his arm raised.

She squeezed the trigger.

The gun jumped in her hands and fell to the floor.

An audible curse, and he grabbed his bicep. She hit him!

A leather boot came down, and she covered her head just in time to deflect the blow. Her weapon was no longer in sight, and she jumped to her feet.

She plowed through a stack of lights and decorations. A cord wrapped around her shoe caused her to trip, but she kept moving.

"I'm going to kill you," the man's voice grumbled.

She stepped to the right and then shoved a tall metal candleholder toward the man.

Silas appeared at the top of the ladder. "Watch out!"

Silas aimed his gun.

The man was right on her heels, and she made a beeline for Silas.

Gunfire exploded.

She squealed and ducked. Strong hands shoved her in the back, causing her to plunge forward. Silas reached out but missed.

Then she was falling over the edge. She landed in a shallow pile of hay at the feet of the longhorn. The cow startled and kicked Kennedy in the thigh before darting to the other side of the pen.

Pain shot through her, but she scrambled to her feet and stumbled to the wooden fence. As her foot fought to find the bottom rung, she glanced back to the loft.

Silas squatted down, and as he leaped, something flew through the air. A knife stuck in the back of his shoulder.

"Put your hands up." A Jarvis County deputy stood at the corner of the barn and had his weapon aimed at the man in the loft.

Kennedy glanced up just long enough to see the attacker drop his weapon. She ran to Silas's side. "Are you okay?"

He grimaced but rolled to his knees. The knife fell to the ground.

"You're bleeding."

Silas struggled to his feet, and the deputy handcuffed the injured assailant. A trickle of blood ran down Silas's back, soaking his shirt. She thought she was going to be sick.

Silas staggered to another deputy who had walked up. "There's another one down in the woods."

Dead? Had Silas killed someone? The danger was surreal. All her life, she'd lived a quiet and sheltered existence. At least the part of her life she remembered.

More sirens sounded as an ambulance pulled up the drive.

The deputy said, "You need to have that cut looked at."

Silas shook his head and motioned for the man to follow. "My partner is seriously injured. He's in my truck."

Kennedy watched as people rushed around, a deputy handcuffed the man that was in the loft, and paramedics helped Ranger Randolph. She overheard one deputy tell another that Glen Winsett was being detained and questioned as he tried to leave the adoption agency. She glanced toward the woods and wrapped her arms around herself. Being a psychologist, she felt the need to help someone, but she didn't know where to start.

Yes, she did. She put a call in to her boss.

Bliss answered on the first ring. "What's going on?"

Kennedy proceeded to give her a quick rundown of all she knew. Silence met her on the other end, making her wonder what her boss was thinking.

"Let me pull Josie and Chandler from the case they're working. They're a few hours out, but I'll get them on the way."

"No," Kennedy snapped. She drew a deep breath. "Listen. They're working on an active abduction case. Chandler has his search-and-rescue dog, which would not benefit me at all. Please don't have them drop what they're doing to help me. The local sheriff's department and the Texas Rangers are helping."

"Do they know where the owner of the adoption agency is right now?"

"Yes, he's being detained at the agency right now."

"Are you certain you're fine? We take care of our own."

Kennedy's heart swelled. Right now, with her world spinning out of control, she needed to hear she belonged. She swallowed down the building emotion. "Thanks, Bliss. I'll let you know if I need anything."

"You do that. And we'll talk when all of this over."

Kennedy clicked off and thought about her boss's words. *We'll talk.* Did she want Kennedy to get help? Like professional help? Hmm. Could be. And as much as she wanted to deny the need, she had never felt at a loss as much as she did right now.

With everyone busy, she stepped over to the large pecan tree and sat in the swing attached to ropes, desiring to stay out of the way. The freezing wind whipped through the yard, and she tugged her jacket tighter. The trees were bare of leaves, and dead grass covered the lawn. Bare and cold. Much like her life. Her daddy struggled with dementia, and now she knew he wasn't even her biological dad. Not that it mattered. Not really. Many people were raised by people other than their biological moms and dads. It was the not knowing that bothered her. Like the rug had been pulled from underneath her protected and secure feet.

Maybe she should feel blessed that her "mom and dad" had loved her. And now she had another mom and brother and sister to get to know. But would she ever feel a part of that family? *Her* family.

She wasn't the only victim. What about Rosa? If her dad was indicted on kidnapping, it would tear their family apart.

Thirty minutes later, Silas made his way back to her. "Thought you'd want to know, Liz is home now."

"That's great." Kennedy's stomach churned at the thought of meeting her as her daughter for the first time. Silas had finally told Liz Kennedy's true identity, for which she was glad.

"Are you ready to go?"

"Where are we going?"

"Not us. You. To your house." He held his hand out to help her up. Gauze and tape stuck out from the collar of his shirt. "With the explosion, I don't want you anywhere near the adoption agency when we go in. If Mr. Winsett doesn't want us finding evidence, there's no telling what he'll do."

That made sense. Although she didn't want to stay out of the way, she realized it was important for Silas and the others to be able to do their jobs without worrying about her safety. "All right. How is the stab wound?"

"I'm fine. Took eight stitches," he said. "I've had much worse."

They walked over to his truck, and as she climbed in, she noted dried blood marred the back seat. "How is Ranger Randolph?"

Silas glanced at her. "He's going to make it." His hoarse voice was filled with worry, even though he tried to hide it. She prayed he was right.

He put his vehicle into gear and headed out of the drive.

"I'm going to my mom Liz's house." She managed not to stumble on the words.

His head jerked as he looked at her. "Are you certain?"

"Yes," she breathed. "We have a lot to talk about."

"I will drop you off."

"No." She put her hand on his. "I'll drive my car. It'll be much quicker for you to get the agency from my house. And I wouldn't mind being alone."

"All right."

Disappointment hovered over her. Somehow, she'd hoped he would argue. That was silly, of course. He'd already made it clear he was going back to work soon and didn't have time for relationships.

As he pulled onto the highway, Silas seemed far away. She hadn't known him long, but she was familiar with men like him. He was feeling so near closing this case, he could taste it. He didn't want distractions.

Was she a distraction? After the case closed, would he go back to his life as a Texas Ranger? Not that she blamed him. Of course, that was his plan. It was his career. He'd come running when she'd yelled for help and had been by her side ever since. He would've done that for anyone.

"Are you okay?"

She startled at his words. "What?"

"You look serious. We'll get to the bottom of this. The deputies are already at the agency, and if there's anything to find, we'll find it. We'll send a Ranger out to Liz's when we're done. Then all this will be over."

All this. Including them? They'd be over? She didn't have time for relationships right now. How could someone start a relationship when they didn't know who they were? What if she didn't like Elizabeth Barclay? Or her family didn't like her?

He pulled into her drive. Her car, slightly crumpled hood and all, sat in her yard. Awkwardness hung in the air like there were things left unsaid.

His cell phone rang, and he quickly answered it. "This is Boone."

She couldn't understand the mumblings of the voice on the other end.

"I'll be right there." He clicked off and turned to her. "The Texas Rangers and local law enforcement are inside. A check into Winsett's financials turned up money from the adoption agency to Victoria Rollins."

That was surprising since it was such a long time ago, but that was good, wasn't it? She could sense the excitement in Silas. "Awesome."

He looked at her straight on. "Did you know Rosa was adopted, too? She was two years old at the time."

"What? Are you sure?" Kennedy couldn't believe that. "Why wouldn't she have told me?"

"Maybe she didn't know."

"Could be…" Her voice trailed off.

"Keep your phone with you," he admonished.

"I will." As soon as the door shut, he took off, no doubt in a hurry to get to the agency for the takedown. She watched until his truck disappeared down the road. As soon as he was out of sight, she climbed into her car.

Concern for Rosa grew. She'd call her friend tomorrow depending on how the investigation with her dad went. This situation was new to Kennedy.

But right now, it was time to meet Elizabeth Barclay for the first time as mother and daughter.

SIXTEEN

Kennedy needed to talk with her mom alone. If Shasta or Dax were there, that would be fine as well.

With so much riding on her shoulders, the trip seemed to fly by. She'd helped people in difficult situations and had learned a long time ago, there was no right or wrong in these circumstances.

Freezing drizzle pinged against the windshield and the wind pushed against her Mini Cooper. Leaves skittered across the road. Even though it was midafternoon, the sky had turned darker. As she pulled into the drive, she tried to determine what words she should say, but nothing came to mind.

Solomon lay on the porch and trotted over to her car, barking.

She parked behind the older car and climbed out. "Oh, hello, Solomon." Would the dog remember her? He thumped his tail in powerful moves, and she patted him on the head. Hurrying up the porch, she rapped on the door. "Liz. Mrs. Barclay..."

Words that sounded like *come in* came to her. Kennedy stepped into the foyer. "It's me, Kennedy." She knew now she was Harper, but she didn't know if she should change the name she'd grown accustomed to. All the lights were off, except something glowed from the living room. "Mrs. Barclay..."

"In here."

Kennedy stepped into the living room and saw her mom sitting in a recliner covered with a colorful quilt. Quietly, she walked over to her. "I hope I'm not interrupting your sleep."

A smile lit on her lips. "Never. Come here."

She did as her mom asked, and the woman took her hand, her eyes glistening. "I'm so glad you're home. Silas told me."

Kennedy swallowed down the lump in her throat. "I'm glad, too." The words came out raspy. She glanced around. "Are you alone? I thought maybe Dax or Shasta would be here. I don't want to intrude."

"It's just me. Dax dropped me off from the hospital, and Shasta is supposed to be here later to bring me supper and spend the night. I told her there was no need because several women from church dropped off meals and put them in the refrigerator."

"Aw. I love it when people help like that."

Her mom glanced at her. "I do, too. But I'd rather be on the giving side of that dish than the receiving. I don't like feeling weak."

Kennedy smiled. "I understand."

"I realize this is a strange situation, but know this, you're always welcome in my home. This family. It must be difficult for you. Look at me."

She turned to the older woman and looked her directly on, at the emotion dancing in her eyes. Her mom took her hands in hers. She started to speak, but then her lips trembled. Finally, she said, "I could just stare at your face all day. You turned out absolutely beautiful. Perfect." She smiled. "I still can't believe you made it home. People tried to ease my pain by trying to convince me you'd died and were in heaven, not to have hope. I'd put on a brave face, but deep down, I knew you were out there. I prayed wherever you were, you were safe and happy."

Kennedy pulled her mom into a hug. For several long moments, they held each other. When they finally released, she swiped tears. "I'm sorry. I had no idea I was even abducted.

I don't have many memories, but I must ask you something."

"What is it?"

"Sometimes I have visions of a black-and-white dog. Did we have one?"

Her mom laughed. "Snoopy."

Kennedy didn't know if it was the emotions or her memory, but the name brought happiness to her.

"From what Silas said, your mom and dad were good to you?" Her forehead wrinkled.

Kennedy caught the concern with the question. "Yes, they were. My mom passed away less than a year ago. We were…close." To be caught between two mothers was more difficult than Kennedy imagined. She didn't want to mar her mother's memory, but also wanted her biological mom to know she loved her, too.

"I'm relieved to hear that. I had no idea who had taken you, but the scenarios were never good. I prayed you were well taken care of. And I'm sorry she passed away, and hope for your well-being, they were not the ones who abducted you. Even though Dax doesn't remember you because he was too young and Shasta wasn't born yet, they always knew of you. Our family had three children. Not two."

The words brought her comfort, but she

knew it was possible her siblings felt different, and their mother simply didn't know it.

"I need you to do something for me."

Kennedy waited for her to continue.

"Look in that chest over there by the fireplace." She pointed to the opposite side of the room.

Kennedy noted a cedar chest and walked to it and raised the lid. A bundle of little girl's clothes, a couple of dolls, and a small pink-and-white tattered quilt lay inside. Her chest tightened. She remembered that quilt. She picked it up and breathed in the musty smell. "I remember this. Did you make this for me?"

Her mom laughed. "I wish. My stitches were never that tiny and straight. Your grandmother, Blanche Harper Wilson, made that for you right after you were born."

"You named me after my grandmother?"

A proud smile crossed her face. "Yes. You were the first grandchild."

Grandparents. "Is she… Are any…"

"Mom passed away seven, almost eight years ago. Horace Wilson, my dad, passed away a year before her. But your daddy's mama is still alive and healthy. She lives in Dallas in a house with her older sister. Both get along fine with little assistance. Besides Dax and Shasta, I've told no one about finding you. I didn't want to get the family's hopes up until I was certain."

With shaky hands, her mom opened the photograph album. The first few pages were of a baby with no hair. "There you are."

Baby pictures. A lifetime of grief passed through Kennedy. Her mom described each picture and what was going on at the time. After numerous images of her first year of life came several of her holding a newborn—Dax. Harper had the huge grin of a proud big sister. Then there was one of her playing with Snoopy. The last page showed Harper in front of a Christmas tree beside a new red tricycle, and the last photo in the book was the same one as in the cold case file.

Her mom closed the book, almost symbolic of Kennedy's life changing forever.

"I'd like for you to have this so you can get to know yourself." Her mom held out the album. "I can have Shasta make copies of the rest of the family photos for you."

"Oh, thank you." She pulled the album against her chest. "I can't tell you what this means to me."

Solomon let out a single bark from outside.

Kennedy exchanged glances with her mom before heading for the front of the house.

A noise sounded by the back door, and she

stopped. Kennedy glanced back to her mom. "Are you expecting someone?"

"No one besides Shasta, and she uses the front door. Could be one of the church ladies."

Maybe that's why Solomon had ceased his barking. As Kennedy walked toward the utility room, she slid the .38 from her back pocket. A glance at the utility window showed a red sports car sitting in the drive—the same one that almost hit Dryden at the hospital.

The back door swung inward with a bang.

A familiar man with a gun stepped inside and aimed directly at Kennedy's chest. She couldn't believe her eyes. Colton Schmidt, Rosa's husband.

Did Silas suspect him?

He shouted. "Drop the gun and get over there beside your mom."

Kennedy's hand shook as she considered not complying. Would Colton really shoot her? Maybe. She couldn't take the chance he'd hurt her mom.

"Hope you enjoyed the little reunion with your mother while it lasted. You should've stopped investigating and none of this would have happened."

He moved closer and through gritted teeth, demanded, "Drop it!"

As Kennedy stared into his fiery eyes, a madman stared back at her.

She released her grip, and her gun fell to the tile.

Silas needed to know what was going on. Even if she reached him, he might not get here in time to help. Kennedy needed to take Colton down herself.

After the bomb squad cleared the Loving Heart Adoption Agency building, Silas and the Texas Rangers moved in. Josie Hunt, an investigator with the Bring the Children Home Project, was with them. Evidently, Bliss had thought Josie would be of more assistance on this case. Everyone spread out into different rooms and began combing the offices for evidence. There was no need to remind the officers to be careful with the evidence and protocol. They all were trained to know what was at stake.

Silas and Dryden, along with two others, combed Winsett's office, where they believed most of the evidence would be. With glove-clad hands, they sifted through the desk and the storage closet. Bare drawers showed thirty minutes later. He wondered if Glen was that neat, or he'd already removed the files.

According to arresting deputies, Winsett

had continued his rants of innocence. Against his lawyer's wishes, the man had stuck to his claim that he had nothing to do the attacks on Liz and Kennedy. But surprising everyone, he confessed to being behind Kennedy's kidnapping. Doubt niggled at Silas as he continued through the files and the man's office. Was it possible the owner didn't orchestrate and pay for the attacks? Who else would have a motive?

Finding a twenty-six-year-old money trail back to Victoria struck Silas as convenient.

Josie came into the room. "There's not much in the secretary's things. Makes me wonder if everything has been cleaned out."

Silas sighed. "Same thing here. But keep searching. It's easy to overlook things, especially trying to hide your tracks for over twenty-six years, before computers were commonplace. Have you found any hard files?"

Dryden held up a key. "Lookee here. It's a key to a warehouse. I could start checking all the local warehouses."

"Are storage facilities listed on the search warrant?" Silas didn't want any excuse for this guy to get off if he was behind the crime.

Dryden smiled. "Sure is."

"I saw a bill to a warehouse in a stack on the secretary's desk," Josie said. "Let me find it again." Several minutes later, she hollered, "Found it."

"Could be where old hard copies were kept. You want to go check it out?"

"You don't have to tell me twice." Luke left the office.

As Silas and Josie searched the area, Silas kept feeling like they were missing something. Glen Winsett. Admitted kidnapper. But why admit to that but not the attacks? Was it because of Victoria's murder? That would get him more time than kidnapping. But at his age, he'd more than likely die in prison.

People came and went. He heard from Chasity, the investigator at the Texas Rangers, who informed him a steady trail of money had been missing from the Loving Heart Adoption Agency for years. Was Glen embezzling from his own company? If not Glen, then who?

Colton, Winsett's son-in-law, could be the one. Or several other people. But Silas's mind returned to the young man. The expensive house. The defensive attitude. He had access to the books. With all the focus on Winsett, no one had been paying attention to the son-in-law.

Silas's phone buzzed. A text from Frank Henry. Dread filled him as he opened the attachment. An image of Verne smiling and holding a whopper of a catfish. Relief from seeing Kennedy's dad seemingly doing well, until his gaze glanced at the message.

Couldn't reach Kennedy, but I knew she'd like to see Verne's catch. Frank.

   Silas's mouth went dry. Why wasn't Kennedy responding to Frank's call? But even as he hit her number and it began to ring unanswered, he knew he'd messed up. He should've kept her by his side. He prayed he wasn't too late.

SEVENTEEN

Kennedy's heart raced as Colton jabbed the gun in her side. But more than that, she feared for her mom. She couldn't lose two moms in one year.

"Get beside the old woman."

Anger boiled within Kennedy, but she knew to be patient and hurried to do as he asked. How would Colton react if she backed him into a corner?

"Who are you?" her mom asked. "What do you want?"

Sweat ran down his face, and his cheeks burned red. "We don't have time for twenty questions. Do as you're told. Barclay, sit on the coffee table."

He didn't make false promises they'd live or wouldn't be hurt. Kennedy helped her mom get up from the recliner and move to the wooden table in the center of the room. Physically, the woman appeared healthy except for the bump on her head. But she didn't know how well her mom could hold up to the stress.

Fury burned in Colton's eyes, and he held out two long zip ties. "Secure her hands behind her back."

"But it'll hurt her. She just got out of the hospital and poses no threat to you." Kennedy glared at him.

He glanced at his watch, and shouted, "Hurry up. I don't care. Just get her hands secured."

Gently she gathered her mom's hands into her lap, the bruises from the IV were still black and large. She fastened the ties without making them too tight.

"You. Get your hands behind you."

Kennedy wanted to refuse but didn't take the chance. She'd make her move when he wasn't watching for it. With a jerk, he pulled her arm behind her, causing pain to shoot through her shoulder. Automatically, she went up on her tiptoes and bent backward to ease the pain. He yanked on them until the plastic dug into her wrists. She didn't give him the satisfaction of begging him to loosen the grip.

"Let's go." Colton gave her mom an unnecessary shove in the back to get her going toward the front door.

It amazed Kennedy that her mom kept her

balance, and she moved quickly for a lady who was just released from the hospital.

"Hurry up." He shoved the end of the barrel into Kennedy's back, the sting painful. To create a buffer, she put herself between Colton and her mom. He opened the door and told them to wait by Kennedy's car.

The drizzle had picked up into a light rain and the skies had grown even darker.

Where was Solomon?

Kennedy glanced around but didn't see him anywhere. He'd been on the porch when she arrived. Nausea swirled in her stomach. Surely Colton hadn't harmed the sweet dog.

Her gaze fell on a white object beside the man's pickup. No! "What did you do to the dog?"

"Don't worry about it."

Colton put her mom in the back seat of the Mini Cooper and then Kennedy. Feeling his hands on her made her want to kick him, but she didn't dare for fear he'd retaliate against her mom. Space between the seat and the back of the front was tight, but they managed to fit.

A second later, he tore up the drive, the windshield wipers beating in rhythm.

Where was Silas? She searched the road, praying to see his truck speeding toward them, but saw no one. When she glanced at her mom, sharp eyes stared back at her.

"Don't worry about me," her mom whispered. "If you can get away, do it."

"I won't leave you."

Her mom shook her head. "I can't lose you again."

Colton hit the brakes, sending them flying forward. Kennedy's head smacked the back of his seat.

"Keep your mouths shut!" Colton's narrowed gaze met Kennedy's in the rearview mirror.

Anger rolled through her, but she kept her thoughts to herself. Why did he take her car? What was his plan?

With the way he was acting, she didn't think he would listen to reason. There had to be a way to get a hold of Silas. Her cell phone was in her front pocket, but with her hands tied behind her, there was no way to reach it. Maybe her mom could help.

Kennedy barely scooted her bottom toward her mom and then leaned away from her. When Liz looked at her, Kennedy mouthed, "Front pocket."

Her mom squinted before realization hit her. She nodded and inched closer.

Colton turned down a dirt road. The trees thickened to form a tunnel over them. Rain continued to fall and sounded like it had picked up even more. Oh no. Kennedy glanced around.

This was the bridge that crossed the Red River. Not again.

They had to get out. Her mom finally reached Kennedy's cell phone, but it fell onto the floorboard. If Colton heard the thump, he didn't appear to care. Her mom bent forward and, and even as they bumped over rough terrain, she snagged the device and passed it to Kennedy.

Colton maneuvered the tiny car around the concrete pole. She wished she'd bought a land yacht instead of her Mini Cooper. In panicky movements, Kennedy hurried to call Silas, but she couldn't see the screen. She jerked her head to her mom, and mouthed, "Call Silas."

As the car pulled to a stop, her mom hit the number.

Colton got out of the car. "Time to go for a little ride."

Not being able to see, she slid the phone into her back pocket and hoped she didn't accidentally turn it off. They had to give Silas time to get here. By her best guess, he was at least twenty minutes away, even if he broke the speed limit.

Colton yelled, "Get out."

Not an easy task with her hands tied behind

her back, but she pressed her head on the back of the driver's seat to give her leverage and climbed out. Colton grabbed her mom's biceps and yanked to get her to her feet. Anger boiled in Kennedy.

Using her head, she rammed him in the chest, but he turned, making it a glancing blow. She stumbled forward and almost lost her balance. A hard slap came down on the back of her head, dropping her to her knees.

"Harper!" Her mom's shrill yell sent chills down her neck.

The woman raced to her side, but Kennedy was afraid he'd hurt the woman she'd just now gotten to know. "I'm okay. Get back."

"Enough. Get up and get into the driver's seat. You, on the passenger side."

Kennedy's mind scrambled with what his plan was. But as realization hit, she suddenly knew. Hoping, praying Silas was listening on the phone, she screamed, "Help us! We're at the Old Carpenter's Bluff Bridge. Colton is going to kill us."

A fist belted her in the jaw, knocking her delirious. "You can be dead when you reach the water. Just keep it up."

Tears filled her eyes, and her head throbbed from the punch. The wooden planks on the bridge seemed to sway. Did he break her jaw?

She worked her mouth and his hand clasped down on her arm. He jerked her to her feet and painfully dragged her to the car. He threw open the door and shoved her inside. Before she knew what he had planned, he withdrew another zip tie from his back pocket and grabbed her foot.

She fought and struggled, but he still managed to get her feet strapped together.

As the out-of-control man grabbed her mother, she prayed. *Please, God, save us. Help Silas get here in time.* But even as she muttered the words, she realized there was simply no time.

Colton shoved her mother into the car and then hit her over the head with a large rock that had been lying on the ground.

Kennedy gasped. "Mom!"

Her mom slumped, and blood trickled down the side of her face. She was out cold. Colton cut her mom's zip tie and flung it to the ground.

Kennedy panicked, grasping for the door handle, hoping to escape. She stood on her knees, trying to maneuver her tied hands. He sprinted around to her side of the vehicle. Just as she latched onto the handle, he yanked open the door.

She fell back to the seat and kicked with her might, pummeling him with her running shoes. Using her feet like she was attacking a punching bag, she fought for her life. With a powerful kick, she connected with his face.

Red fury engulfed his cheeks. He brought the rock back and swung, connecting with her thigh—the same one the longhorn had kicked. Instinctively, she grabbed for her leg, yelled, and then everything went blurry. Before she could protect her herself, he hit her again, this time in the head, and pain exploded. Fireflies danced before her eyes. She tried to keep her balance, but it was no use. Light faded and darkness overtook her.

Please. Don't pass out. I must stay awake.

She fell against the console and even as her eyes opened, her world spun. Somewhere far away, she felt her arms being jerked, and then they were free. She fought the fuzzy sensation, but also welcomed it. If only the agony would stop.

Her legs were crammed inside the car, and then she was moving. Or was her brain still spinning? She squinted. The black clouds moved.

A dull thumping sounded as if the car was running over something.

She fought to unscramble her thoughts, and her body begged to close her eyes and rest. But Colton wanted to kill her and her mom. She couldn't sleep. Not yet.

She forced her eyes open. Rain ran down the windshield. *Thump. Thump.*

The car *was* moving and slowly gaining speed!

She tried to sit up, and pain instantly stabbed her head. Oh… Nausea swirled through her insides, threatening to make her vomit. Not thinking clearly, she grabbed the steering wheel to help her sit up, and the car jerked to the right.

A high-pitched scraping had her yanking the wheel back to the left. Her foot—still tied to the other one—slammed on the brake, but the sound of squealing tires filled the air.

What in the world?

A glance at the gas pedal showed a rock weighing it down. *Oh no.*

The bumper on the passenger side hooked the metal railing and turned.

As blood continued to trickle down the side of her head, she finally got her feet to cooperate. She kicked at the rock, trying to dislodge it, but instead, the car picked up speed. The Mini Cooper moved across the decrepit bridge farther away from the land and would soon be over the Red River.

She had survived on the ATV, but Silas had been there to help. And her mom hadn't moved. "Mom. Mom. Wake up!"

Thump. Thump. Thump. The sounds became faster. Up ahead, the boards were missing. Kennedy wouldn't be able to save herself this time. She'd be better off to drive off the bridge now where the river wasn't as deep instead of waiting. A gap in the railing appeared to her left, and she jerked the wheel toward it. In one swift move, the car drove through the opening, and free-fell.

Bam!

Water shot into the air.

Kennedy's head slammed into the dash, and her mom smashed into her shoulder. And then they were floating. Even though she'd tried to make it crash over shallow water, the car was still being carried away.

She grabbed her mom's hand and squeezed.

If she was going to die, she wished she would've told Silas how much he meant to her.

EIGHTEEN

Boom!

Silas's windshield exploded just as he sped up to the concrete barrier. He crouched down, slammed his truck into Park and jumped out. He landed on his side and rolled to a stop. With his gun in hand, he searched for the source. Someone ran along the tree line away from the bridge.

Red caught his eye, and he looked to the river.

Kennedy's Mini Cooper! It bobbed in the water and floated down the river.

His heart constricted as he climbed to his feet. The man had disappeared.

Tires on gravel sounded behind him. He glanced over his shoulder to see a man with a bloodhound, and Dryden running his way, but he didn't slow as he sprinted along the shoreline. The rain lightened. Twice his boots slid on the muddy banks.

"Silas!"

His adrenaline pumped faster at the sound of Kennedy's voice. The car swirled and leaned to the side as it caught on a sandbar. There were no falls in the river, and the depth tended to be eight to ten feet deep in the middle, and shallower toward the banks. Because of recent rains, the current flowed swiftly. A railroad bridge supported by concrete pillars loomed ahead. If the car dislodged and picked up speed, it would be like hitting a brick wall if it rammed one of the columns.

He sprinted and then dove into the water, swimming at an angle toward Kennedy. The current moved more rapidly than he anticipated, and it dragged him under. A fallen bare tree moved swiftly in front of him. Large branches threatened. He slowed to let it pass, but a broken limb snagged his arm, catching his shirt and pulling him along. He gulped water and went under.

Bubbles gurgled, and the tree rolled, taking him with it. He'd always been an excellent swimmer but had never maneuvered in these conditions.

The concrete piers were getting closer.

Kennedy's car continued to move but hung up on a sandbar. The gap was closing. His body was tiring fast and with pure determination, he kicked off from the tree, releasing himself.

He swam for the car. Just as it started to move again, he reached it and grabbed hold of the bumper and pulled himself onto the hood. Liz was inside the car. Thankfully, Kennedy already had the window down. "Hang on."

The water swirled around them. There was no avoiding the railroad bridge. "I need you to get out. Hurry." Kennedy scurried out of her seat. Wet blood stained the side of her face, and anger rolled inside him.

They were getting closer. Liz was white as a sheet and trying to get out but struggled with the door. Silas climbed across the hood and slid inside the open window. He picked her up and leaned outside the opening, trying to swing her up to safety. Kennedy grabbed her, and they pitched the woman up.

No more time. "Jump into the water."

He dove outside the window just as the car smashed into the concrete. He surfaced and found Kennedy and Liz, clinging to each other. Liz fought to stay above water but dragged Kennedy under.

He caught Kennedy by the arm and pulled her up. "Get to the pillar." When she argued, he said, "I've got your mother. Go."

His jeans weighed him down and the water

was freezing, but pure adrenaline gave him the energy to tear his neighbor from the clutches of the flow and roll her to her back. "I've got you, Liz. You can quit fighting." Wrapping his arm around her shoulders, he hauled her toward the pillars, and he snagged one of the metal supports. Liz clung to him.

Kennedy's face was pale, and her lips turned blue.

"Hang on!" Dryden's voice carried to them from up above on the railway bridge. "Chandler is on his way."

Silas's arms shook from exhaustion, and he didn't know how much longer he could hold on. If he was this spent, how was Kennedy hanging on after she'd been fighting with Colton?

The putt putt of a motor sounded on the water. He looked up to see a fishing boat pushing toward them. A minute later, the man and his bloodhound pulled along beside them. "Get in."

"Chandler, I'm so glad Bliss sent you."

Once all three of them were in the small craft, Silas asked, "Did Colton get away?"

Chandler shook his head. "Deputy Trumble and another deputy had him disarmed and handcuffed."

"I'm surprised they got here so fast."

"They got a tip from Rosa, the man's wife."

Silas turned to Kennedy and Liz. His heart constricted. Both women shivered and clung to each other, Kennedy's arm draped over her mom's shoulder. Despite the critical situation, Kennedy continued to display her concern for others.

He'd tried to keep from falling for her. He truly had. Somewhere along the way, she'd wormed her way into his life.

Way to protect your heart, Boone.

Kennedy woke in a hospital bed under a warm blanket. What? Why was she here? Then she remembered visiting with her mom, Colton showing up and the river. She glanced around the room, and her gaze lit on the clock on the wall. The numbers read four twenty-three. Three or four hours must've passed since Silas had rescued them.

A quick survey of the room showed she was alone. Where was her mom? Her mom had fought the frigid waters but must be as exhausted as she. After spending several days in the hospital, weakness would make her condition more serious.

If hadn't been for Silas and Chandler, there was no doubt neither of them would've survived.

"You're awake."

She glanced up at his voice and smiled. Stubble lined his jaw, and his eye took her in. His shirt hung untucked, and his dark hair was a mess. No one had ever looked more handsome in her life.

"How are you feeling?"

"Warm." She hit the control on the bed and raised it to a sitting position and ran her fingers through her hair. "I'm certain I look a mess."

"You look absolutely beautiful." He shoved a chair next to the bed and sat. Concern swirled in his eye. He drew Kennedy's hand into his. "Seriously? Are you feeling okay?"

The simple action wreaked havoc on her already emotional heart. The gesture felt right and brought comfort. "Yeah. I think I could sleep for three days." She smiled, and then she sobered. "How's my mom?"

"Just fine. Fussing that the doctor hadn't released her already. She's tough as a boot." Silas grazed a finger across her hand. "I just came downstairs from seeing Ranger Randolph. He's out of surgery and the doctor says he's going to make it."

"That's wonderful" She smiled before it faded. "What about Solomon? Has anyone checked on the dog? He was laying on the ground when we left. So help me, that maniac better not have—"

"The big guy is fine," Silas interrupted. "Shasta called when she got to your mom's place and found him dopey but moving around. Evidently Colton shot him with a tranquilizer."

"Oh,that's a relief. You really think of lot of my mom, don't you?"

"She's a fine lady. And yes, I do." He gave her hand a squeeze.

"I like her, too. What happened to Colton? Did I hear Dryden say he'd been arrested?"

Silas released her hand and sat up straight. "Yeah. He's lawyered up, but it won't do any good."

"I don't understand. Why did he want to kill me? He was too young to have anything to do with my kidnapping."

"We still need to dig through the evidence, but it seems he didn't know about the kidnapping until Victoria Rollins left Harper's cold case file on Winsett's desk. Colton found it. In Glen's copy, there was a note saying she was coming clean and wanted to ease her guilt of her part of the kidnapping years ago, and that she planned to let you know."

"But what did the kidnapping have to do with Colton? I still don't see a connection."

"Colton's a greedy fellow. Apparently, he

positioned himself to take over the Loving Heart Adoption Agency when his daddy-in-law retires. Also hoped to inherit the company upon his death. He was embezzling from the company and racking up a lot of debt. We can't prove this yet, but we believe he started digging into the files when he learned Victoria kidnapped and sold you. We're still not certain if Victoria came up with the kidnapping scheme on her own, or if she was paid to do it. Colton found out that Rosa was also adopted. If Rosa learned the truth, she might divorce herself from her parents and look for her biological parents. Colton could kiss the inheritance bye-bye. He worked fast to frame Glen for the attacks in hopes the authorities would arrest Winsett, or better yet, kill Winsett. Not very smart, but he's been obsessed with taking over the company and thought he could speed it up with Winsett in jail. You want to hear the clincher?"

"By the gleam in your eye, I'm not certain."

"Colton's first wife died in a tragic accident. She drove off a bridge late at night, and he inherited several hundred thousand dollars of life insurance money."

Her mouth dropped open. "I didn't even know he was married before. Makes me wonder if Rosa found out. Might explain why she seemed nervous around her husband. Poor Rosa. Wait. Was she kidnapped, too?"

"Probably. With Colton in custody, Winsett is talking. He admits the first year the adoption agency opened, there were three children who were victims of abduction, but he hasn't said who was behind the crimes. Cora, his wife, claims she didn't know that Rosa or any of the children were taken by illegal means, and Glen agreed she had no part or knowledge of any crime."

Kennedy swallowed as she thought about the situation. "Sounds like Glen kept a lot of secrets. And now he's in danger of losing his family." Her thoughts went back to how Rosa seemed timid. "If Rosa didn't know of her husband's past dealings, she must've sensed it."

"Maybe firsthand. She'll be needing a good friend in the coming months."

"I'll be here for her."

"I knew you would." He again tucked her hand into his and gave it a peck.

She stared into Silas's face and absorbed every precious detail. "So, are you saying my parents didn't have anything to do with my kidnapping?"

"It looks that way. I don't know why your parents didn't tell you about your adoption. You could ask your dad, but I'm not sure that's a good idea."

"I might leave that one alone. My parents loved me, and they must've had their reasons."

Her world felt right with Silas by her side. Having someone to depend on wasn't a bad thing. "I couldn't believe my eyes when I saw you standing on the bridge. I don't know how you got there so fast but thank you for coming to me and my mom's rescue."

"I had just learned of Colton's possible embezzlement, and Frank Henry sent me a text of your dad's catfish when he couldn't get hold of you. I knew you would've answered that call. I was already on my way to Liz's when I received your call." His eye connected with hers. "I know we haven't known each other very long as adults, but I'd like to change that. I kind of like you." The cute cleft in his cheek lit up.

She laughed. "You kind of like me?"

"Just a little." His fingers formed a C and then he stretched his hands wide. "More like this."

"I sort of like you, too." Her eyes glistened in the teasing.

His expression fell into seriousness. "I love you, Kennedy." She started to speak, but he held up his hand. "Let me finish. I'm not very good at expressing myself, so I need to get this out. You amaze me. Somehow, you loved and cared for two sets of parents. You've offered forgiveness freely. I'm not talking as some guy who feels bad for letting his young neighbor get abducted at a park while he watched helplessly. When I received your call for help today, and I didn't know if I could make it in time, I prayed. Prayed harder and more sincerely than ever before. You make me a better man. I don't want to lose you."

She swallowed. "For a man who doesn't express himself well, you sure did a grand job. I love you, too, Silas." When he leaned over and gently pressed his lips to hers, she had never felt such gratitude for having so many people love her in her life.

EPILOGUE

Six months later

The early summer sun warmed Kennedy's back as she planted the last cypress tree in the freshly plowed soil and patted the dirt to make sure it wouldn't topple. Almost two acres of pastureland had been plowed and an irrigation system installed. It would take three to six years before the trees were ready for harvest, which meant more acres would be taken in for the farm to have a continuous supply of trees.

She glanced up and looked around. Where had her husband run off to? He'd been preoccupied the last couple of days, and she knew he was up to something.

They got married in April in his grandfather's barn, and she'd never been happier. Even her dad was doing better after his doctor prescribed a new treatment. Dad occasionally had trouble recalling something, but nothing compared to the struggles from previous months. He continued to live on his own, and Kennedy didn't know how much longer that would last. Silas offered to let her dad move in with them, and when the time came, she was good with that.

The Barclays were a large clan, and Kennedy was still getting acquainted with everyone. In so many ways, it was like Dax and Shasta had always been a part of her life, their bond instant. Shasta had two daughters, ages three and four, and Kennedy loved playing aunt.

Colton Schmidt was arrested for the murder of Victoria Rollins, and the attempted murder of Kennedy and her mom. He was sentenced to life in prison. The statute of limitations prevented Glen Winsett from being charged with kidnapping. He and his wife separated, and Cora was helping Rosa search for her biological parents in hopes of reunifying them. The family was going to counseling. Kennedy prayed for them every day, knowing that God can help heal deep wounds.

"Looking good."

"Thanks." She glanced at Silas, dirt covering his jeans, his Stetson riding low on his head, his hands clad in leather gloves, and his patch gone. He received a clean bill of health and had returned to work. Her heart still ran wild at the sight of her husband. But more than his good looks, he was the kindest man she'd ever known.

"I want to show you something."

The grin on her husband's face made her curious. She got to her feet and dusted off her hands and knees. "Where have you been? You've been missing the last couple of hours."

He jerked his head. "Come on. You'll see."

She followed him across the newly planted grove to her mom's land and through the towering trees her dad had planted years ago. Her heart felt light and full of life.

When she came to the clearing, her breath was sucked from her. Her dad's Farmall tractor sported a new red paint job, and Christmas lights twinkled around the tires, making it look like they were moving. "Oh, Silas. It's beautiful."

"You like it? You really don't mind?"

"Mind? Of course not. It's just how I remember it." They had already discussed that this holiday season they could have cut trees trucked in and start building the business before their trees were large enough to cut. It'd take a few years to build the customer base, but many still remembered coming here years ago and were excited the farm would be reopened.

"That's the most precious sight. Wade would be so proud."

Kennedy glanced up to see her mom standing with Solomon at her side and her hand over her mouth. Tears glistened in her eyes. "Mom, it does my soul good to hear my daddy would like it."

"He loved the farm and would love what you two are doing with it. I'll leave you alone."

After she walked away with Solomon, Silas took Kennedy's hands into his own. "I talked to my dad this morning."

Kennedy's heart stilled. Was that good news? "How did it go?"

"We're meeting for lunch at a burger joint. I'd like for you to be with me."

She realized this was a big moment for Silas. Just reaching out was a huge step, and she prayed it went well. "I think you'd be better off without me. Give you and your dad time to talk."

"Nonsense. I want you by my side. You're my wife. If it weren't for you, I never would've had the courage to call him."

She heard the pleading in his voice. "All right. I'll go. I was just thinking how everything turned out good with my family. I found love with so many people, and I want you to have that with yours."

"I knew I could count on you." He pulled her into his arms and captured her lips with his. "I love you."

* * * * *

If you liked this story from Connie Queen, check out her previous Love Inspired Suspense books:

Justice Undercover
Texas Christmas Revenge
Canyon Survival

Available now from Love Inspired Suspense! Find more great reads at www.LoveInspired.com.

Dear Reader,

Thank you for joining me on Silas and Kennedy's journey.

   While investigating a cold case, Kennedy realizes she may be the kidnapping victim from years ago, and someone doesn't want her to learn the truth. Being a psychologist, she's used to helping others, and struggles to ask for assistance. After multiple attacks, she has no choice but to lean on Silas, our hero.

   What about you? Are you hesitant to ask for help even when needed? I think we all want to be independent and sometimes have trouble admitting we need others. I hope you find comfort in the way Kennedy and Silas learn from each other and put their faith in God.

   I love to hear from readers. You can find me on Facebook at www.facebook.com/queenofheartthrobbingsuspense, or keep up with my latest news and books on my website at www.conniequeenauthor.com.

Many thanks,
Connie Queen